THE
JANUARY
STARS

THE JANUARY STARS

KATE CONSTABLE

ALLEN&UNWIN
SYDNEY · MELBOURNE · AUCKLAND · LONDON

First published by Allen & Unwin in 2020

Allen & Unwin
83 Alexander Street
Crows Nest NSW 2065
Australia
Phone: (61 2) 8425 0100
Email: info@allenandunwin.com
Web: www.allenandunwin.com

A catalogue record for this
book is available from the
National Library of Australia

ISBN 978 1 76052 502 6

For teaching resources, explore www.allenandunwin.com/resources/for-teachers

Cover and text design by Debra Billson
Cover images by Shutterstock: cut-out by TAW4; running girl by Igogosha;
girl and man by kintomo; tree by Emir Simsek
Set in 11/16 pt Sabon by Midland Typesetters, Australia
This book was printed in February 2020 by McPherson's Printing Group, Australia

10 9 8 7 6 5 4 3 2 1

For Bill and Jan, who lived it.

I

Even if Clancy had heard the phone ring, she wouldn't have answered it. Clancy didn't like talking to strangers, especially not on the phone.

So the message sat blinking on the machine for a whole day before Harriet, Clancy's mother, discovered it. And then all hell broke loose.

'But you must have heard the phone!' said Harriet.

'I didn't!' insisted Clancy.

'No one rings land lines anymore. She probably thought it was a scammer,' said her younger brother, Bruno, helpfully.

'She's in another world.' Her older sister, Tash, was scornful. 'She wouldn't notice if the whole building blew up.'

'Were you reading, Clance?' asked her father, Tim, hopefully. He was a teacher, and he still dreamed that at least one of his children would develop a love of books.

Harriet hadn't heard the phone because she was out at work. Tim hadn't heard it because he was at school, preparing for the new term that was about to start, and then at a rehearsal with his jazz band.

Bruno hadn't heard it because he had been on the computer all day, wearing headphones. He was in trouble for that now, because he was only supposed to have two hours of computer time a day, even during the summer holidays.

'You can't blame me,' said Tash. 'I was at the oval playing footy with Az and Miranda. I wasn't even here.'

'You should have been.' Harriet glared at Tash over the rims of her red spectacles, the ones she wore in court to make witnesses feel uncomfortable when she cross-examined them. 'You know I don't like you going out and leaving the little ones alone when your father and I aren't home.'

'Nine's not little!' protested Bruno. 'It's virtually double figures.'

'Clancy's old enough to be in charge, isn't she?' said Tim mildly. 'She's starting high school in a couple of weeks.'

'Four weeks and three days.' Clancy gave her father a reproachful look. She was trying not to think about high school until she absolutely had to.

'This is so unfair!' cried Tash. 'I'm the one who's out in the fresh air, doing physical exercise, and I'm the one who gets yelled at?'

'Hey!' said Tim. 'No shouting at your mother.'

'I don't need you to defend me, thank you, Tim,' said Harriet crisply.

Clancy's stomach churned. She couldn't bear it when her family argued, the words swirling and banging off the walls like a swarm of trapped insects. At least when they were all staring silently at their various devices, lost in their individual universes, there was no shouting.

Then Harriet turned on her. 'Tell me the truth, Clancy. You heard the phone ring, but you were too scared to answer it, weren't you? For God's sake! You should have grown out of that by now.'

'I didn't hear it,' faltered Clancy. 'I was...thinking.'

Tash rolled her eyes. Bruno burst into unkind laughter. Even Tim shook his head. Clancy felt her face burn. Why hadn't she just said she was reading? Then at least Dad would have stuck up for her.

But it was true, she really had been thinking. She'd started re-watching *Cosmos* on the iPad (streaming it illegally, which Harriet would definitely disapprove of), and then she'd got stuck on the idea of the endlessly expanding universe.

Endlessly. Expanding. All those stars, all those galaxies, rushing away from each other into the cold, silent, empty dark. Everything falling apart. Forever. Energy leaking away into nothing. Order collapsing into chaos, inevitably, irreversibly. This process, Neil deGrasse Tyson informed her, was called *entropy*, and it was Clancy's new least favourite idea.

But Harriet would never understand that Clancy hadn't picked up the phone because she was worrying about entropy.

The call had been from their uncle Mark. Clancy couldn't remember the last time she'd seen him, except in photographs, and at Nan's funeral. But he was Tim's brother, and he was in trouble. Mark had always been wild; but never as wild as this.

'I didn't even know he was in New Zealand,' said Tash.

'No one did,' murmured Tim.

Bruno bounced on the couch. 'Is Mark going to jail? Are we related to a criminal?'

Clancy asked cautiously, 'So, what has he done, exactly?'

'He broke into a zoo and let all the animals out.' Tash folded her arms. 'So juvenile.'

'It was an aviary, and he released the birds,' said Tim. 'Some kind of environmental protest, something about endangered wetlands. He meant well.'

'There was property damage, too,' said Harriet. '*Extensive* property damage, allegedly.'

'No one was hurt,' said Tim. 'Don't make it sound worse than it is.'

Harriet snorted. 'He's been arrested. How much worse do you want it to be?'

2

Harriet made decisions quickly; they had lost too much time already. She and Tim would fly to New Zealand to rescue Mark: Harriet because she was a lawyer; Tim because he was Mark's brother and the one Mark had called for help.

'You're the only one Mark's ever listened to,' said Harriet.

'Apart from our father,' said Tim. 'But—'

He didn't need to finish the sentence. They all knew that Pa couldn't help with anything anymore.

'New Zealand, cool,' said Tash. 'About time you guys took us overseas.'

'You can't all come,' said Harriet. 'Far too expensive at such short notice. Just Bruno.'

For once, Clancy and Tash were united.

'*Bruno*?'

'Why Bruno?'

'Because he's a boy? He is such a spoilt brat!' Clancy scowled at her brother.

'Why can't I go? I never get to do anything!' cried Tash.

Tim put up one hand. 'It's nothing to do with being a boy. It's because he's the youngest. You two are mature enough to manage. We're trusting you.'

Bruno chanted, 'I'm going to New Zilland. I'm going to New Zilland.'

'Dad! Bruno's being racist,' called Clancy.

'Fine, go to New Zilland.' Tash shrugged. 'I'll stay with Az.'

Clancy began to panic. 'What about me? You can't leave me at home all by myself!'

'Everybody out!' cried Harriet. 'Tim, will you clear the room of children, please? I need to make some phone calls.'

'Clear the court for Her Honour,' said Tim.

Harriet gave him a sharp look. 'Sarcasm is not helpful at this point. And if you were capable of organising yourself and your idiot brother, I wouldn't have to—'

Clancy didn't wait to be cleared. She ran to the small bedroom she shared with Bruno, and slammed the door on everyone. But it was no use. This apartment was too small for arguments: the thin walls shook with angry voices and the air was sour with resentment like the smell of burned food.

Clancy huddled in the corner of the bunk. She couldn't lose herself in *Cosmos* again because she'd left the iPad in the living room. Instead she listened to Harriet's clear, firm voice as she booked flights and hotels, and arranged emergency leave from work. 'Shouldn't take more than a couple of days,' Clancy heard her say. 'Lucky it's summer and there's not much on, and my husband's on holidays, of course, until school goes back – yes, he's a music teacher—'

Staring at the luminous stars she'd stuck to the bottom of the bunk, Clancy wondered, since Dad was on holidays and Mum didn't have many cases to attend to, why hadn't they all gone away somewhere together? Other families went on trips to Bali, to Disneyland, camping at the beach. But her family never did. Somehow it was never convenient. Mum was in the middle of an important case, or Dad was playing at a festival, or Tash was going on a training camp with her football club, or Bruno was doing a drama workshop.

Anyway, they would never agree on the best place to go. Tash loved camping, but Clancy hated it. Tim liked music, but Harriet preferred history. Bruno liked swimming, but Harriet hated the beach. Clancy wanted to go to the desert so she could see the stars, but that would be too hot for Tim.

There had been that one awkward trip to Sydney a couple of years ago, to visit Po Po, their Chinese grandmother, and their uncles. But the uncles had been at work all the time, and Po Po and Harriet didn't get on very well. Tash explained to Clancy and Bruno, 'Po Po's not happy about Mum marrying Dad.'

'Because he's not Chinese?' said Clancy.

'No! Po Po's not racist. It's because he's a music teacher.'

'Well, that's dumb,' said Bruno.

Anyway, they hadn't gone back to Sydney.

Lucky for Mark we were home, thought Clancy...

...and now would be the perfect moment for Hagrid to arrive on the doorstep to whisk her off to Hogwarts, or the Doctor in the TARDIS. But exciting things like that would never happen to her. If Hagrid did knock on the door, he'd probably be looking for Tash...

Right on cue, there was a tap on the bedroom door, and Clancy jumped. 'Come in.'

But it wasn't Hagrid or the Doctor; only Tim. He perched on the end of the bottom bunk, and Clancy sat up. 'Have you found someone to stay with me?'

'What? Oh, no, you're not staying here. You and Tash are going to Polly's.'

There was a pause.

'Polly. You know, my sister, Polly?'

'I know who she *is*,' said Clancy. 'But we don't *know* her.'

'Of course you know her. You've met her loads of times.'

'Twice, maybe. At Christmas. And all she said was, "how's school?" I can't stay with her.'

'You'll be fine. Tash will be there.'

'Dad, *please* not Polly! Isn't there someone else?'

Tim sighed. 'Sorry, Clancy, I know it's not ideal. I sympathise, but we tried everyone else we could think of. It's such short notice. Polly's family, so she couldn't

8

say no! That's a joke,' he added quickly. But Clancy knew it wasn't, not completely.

Tim went on, 'Our flight leaves first thing tomorrow morning. Mum thinks we'll be able to sort everything out in a couple of days. Hopefully.'

Bruno zoomed in, singing. 'I'm flying to New Zeeeland, and you're going to Pol-ly's, porrible Polly, porrible Polly—'

'Hey!' Tim frowned. 'Bit of respect for your aunt, please.'

Tash thrust her head round the doorway. 'If it's only for a couple of days, why can't we stay here by ourselves? We're responsible – well, I am. Don't forget I can start learning to drive next year.'

'Not in my car!' yelled Harriet from the bedroom.

'And you know Clancy's too much of a wuss to do anything risky—'

'That's true,' said Clancy humbly.

'I'm *trustworthy*,' said Tash. 'I'm not *wild*. Not like Mark…'

Tim stood up abruptly and left the room.

'Too soon?' Tash called after him. 'Too soon.' She shrugged at Clancy.

'Can you get out of my room?' said Clancy.

'It's Bruno's room, too. Bruno, do you mind if I stay in your room?'

Bruno had scrambled up to his top bunk and was rummaging for his most precious Lego creations to pack for New Zealand. 'I don't care.'

'Get out, get out, get out!'

Clancy pushed her sister out of the room and slammed the door. Bruno peered down as she leaned against the door to stop Tash breaking back in.

'How are you going to cope when it's just you and her?' he said. 'When you're at Polly's and I've flown to *New Zealand*?'

Clancy didn't answer. She had no idea.

★ ★ ★

Their protests were no use. Before the day was over, Tash and Clancy had packed their bags and Tim had driven them across the city to their aunt's house. They'd never been there before, and Clancy briefly entertained hopes of a mysterious mansion with a portal to a parallel world, or a tower lookout with a telescope, or at least a shabby cheerful cottage with a sprawling garden and a multitude of pets.

Harriet had always said they couldn't possibly have pets in their inner suburban flat.

But Polly's place turned out to be a narrow, boring townhouse in a row of narrow, boring townhouses, in a narrow, boring suburb called Tutt's Flat, where Clancy and Tash knew no one and there was nothing to do.

Polly peered anxiously into the car. 'Do you want to come in for a cup of tea, Tim? Coffee? A beer?'

'No, thanks.' Tim didn't like beer. 'Better get going. Early start tomorrow.' There was an awkward pause. 'Thanks for taking the girls, Polly. We really appreciate it.'

'No problem!' cried Polly, her voice high and nervous. 'Happy to help! Any time! Give my love to Mark! Good luck!'

Tash stumped inside as Clancy watched their father drive away. When the car vanished at the end of the street, she turned to climb the steps into Polly's house and her eye was caught by the pinprick of a star just above the roofline. It shone steadily, silver against the deep blue velvet of the sky, and Clancy felt obscurely comforted.

Their aunt Polly was no Hagrid, Nanny McPhee, or even Mary Poppins. She was single and had no children of her own, no sense of humour that Clancy could discover, and she spoke to the girls in a brittle, falsely cheery voice that put their nerves on edge.

'We're just people, you know?' complained Tash, privately, in the cramped spare room they were sharing.

'Not alien life forms,' agreed Clancy.

It was clear that their aunt was just as uncomfortable with them as they were with her. Polly rushed off early in the morning to her work as an orthodontist ('Teeth don't take holidays!' she said, in her special bright voice) and rushed back home in the evening with bags of takeaway food.

She smiled nervously at them over Thai green curry, showing her own brilliantly white and even teeth. 'Are you having a good time, girls? Not too bored? Why don't you go to the movies tomorrow? Or the arboretum?'

Tash looked up. 'The aquarium?'

'No, no!' Polly tittered. 'That's fish. The arboretum is a tree collection.'

'So, a park?' Tash rolled her eyes. 'That sounds fascinating.'

'Of course, you're right, that was a silly idea,' agreed Polly. 'Sorry.'

They lapsed into silence. Clancy pushed her food around her plate.

'Is it all right? Too spicy? We can try the other restaurant next time. Unless...you do like Thai, don't you?'

Clancy muttered, 'It's fine.'

Tash said, 'Clancy hates curry. She hates everything, pretty much, except cereal.'

'Oh! I didn't realise...But you know, cereal is not good for your teeth...I'll pick some up tomorrow.'

'It's *fine*.' Clancy scowled at Tash and scooped up a forkful of plain rice. Of course Tash would eat anything. Tash loved spices. Tash would try any bizarre culinary experiment that Tim served up – eel or brussels sprouts or blue cheese sauce, food that any normal person would gag at.

At least the food Polly provided wasn't as weird as that. In fact, Clancy didn't mind being at Polly's too much, as she had good wi-fi. Lucky Clancy had remembered to bring the iPad. She lay on the couch in Polly's neat, dim, apparently-never-used living room, mildly bored, watching videos for hours, while Tash prowled the hot streets outside like a tiger on the loose, hunting for entertainment. The *couple of days* that Harriet and Tim had promised to be away stretched into three, then four.

By Wednesday night, Polly had become almost as restless as Tash. At last, reluctantly, guiltily, their aunt confessed that she had plans of her own. She had booked a trip to Sydney, weeks ago, to spend a few days with friends. 'I'm supposed to leave tomorrow...But of course I can't go while you're still here, can I?'

Polly has friends? thought Clancy in genuine surprise.

'You should totally go,' said Tash immediately. 'Don't worry about us.'

'Is there any chance your parents might be back by tomorrow night? Or even Friday might be all right, I suppose...?'

'Definitely,' said Tash promptly. 'Last night Dad said the end of the week, for sure.'

'I don't want them to rush back because of me. I did promise to look after you.'

'You'd only be leaving us for one night, tops.'

'Are you sure you'd be okay?' It felt as if Polly were begging for their permission. 'I don't get away very often, and I was looking forward to it...'

Clancy said nothing, but she didn't want Polly to leave them all alone, not even for one night.

'I promise I won't throw a party or anything,' said Tash.

'Oh! I didn't even think of that!' Polly screwed up

her face anxiously. 'But I know I can trust you. If you're *absolutely* sure…'

'Absolutely,' said Tash.

And Polly went.

'I can't believe she actually did that,' marvelled Clancy later, still shocked, even long after everything that happened next.

'Maybe not her best call,' agreed Tash.

★ ★ ★

Early on Thursday morning, just before Polly dived into her Uber to the airport, she said, 'Will you do me a favour, girls, if you get a chance? Go and visit your grandfather. I usually pop in before work on a Thursday.'

Tash was offended. 'I was going to visit Pa anyway. I've already been. Twice.'

'Clancy?' Polly hovered with one foot in the car. 'I know Pa would love to see you.'

Clancy squirmed. 'Yeah, okay,' she muttered.

The car door slammed, and Polly was driven away.

Tash threw her arms in the air. 'Free at last!' She pointed at Clancy. 'And you're coming to visit Pa today. You promised.'

'Can't I stay here?' pleaded Clancy.

'If you don't come, maybe I will throw that party after all—'

'Tash! You wouldn't!'

'Not if you come and see Pa.'

'Okay, okay.'

Clancy slumped against the doorway while Tash stalked inside. It was so early that a single star still lingered low in the dawn sky. Was it the same star she'd seen before, the night Tim left them here? *It must be Venus*, thought Clancy, the morning star that was actually not a star at all, but a planet...Morning star, evening star, a steady silver light that would become invisible when the sun rose.

But of course Venus would still be there. It struck Clancy for the first time, with a pleased, private sense of discovery, that the stars didn't really 'come out' when night fell; they were there all the time. It was just that the sun's light was so bright that you couldn't see them anymore.

It made Clancy wonder what else might be lurking around, invisible to the eye. Just because you couldn't see something didn't prove it didn't exist. You couldn't see gravity, but that was real...so maybe all kinds of things like ghosts and magic and UFOs were real, too...

A prickle ran down Clancy's spine, and she hurried inside after her sister.

4

Clancy trailed slowly behind Tash as they walked to The Elms, the aged care home where Pa had lived since he had his stroke, four years ago. The sun was hot and high in the sky, and the shadows of the tree trunks made crisp stripes across the pavement. Clancy loved Pa, of course, and she wanted to see him. But she hated going to The Elms.

That was because Pa hated The Elms, too.

Before his stroke, before Nan died, Pa had had a great life. He and Nan had travelled all around Australia finding rare birds for Nan to photograph and Pa to record in his observation notebook. Now Nan's photographs and Pa's notebooks were in boxes, shut in a cupboard in Pa's room. He didn't often take them out. There weren't many opportunities for birdwatching at The Elms. There was a canary in a cage, but you could only note that once.

The Elms was only a few blocks away from Polly's house. That was the main reason why Pa had ended up living here: so it would be easy for Polly to drop in and see him. But Polly worked long hours and Pa went to bed early, and now Polly only visited her father a couple of times a week.

Tash strode briskly ahead. If Clancy hadn't been with her, she probably would have run, despite the heat. Tash loved to run; she played football; she was always in a hurry. Clancy preferred to take things slowly. And carefully. Watching her sister's back disappearing down the driveway of The Elms, Clancy felt both guilty and annoyed.

Clancy dawdled as Tash punched in the security code and held the automatic sliding doors open impatiently. She arrived at the doorway just in time to see a ginger cat slink out and vanish into the bushes.

'Tash! You let the cat out!'

'Only because you're so *slow*.' Tash marched up to the shrubbery. 'Hey, cat! Come here!'

'Don't yell like that, you'll scare him.' Clancy peered through the leaves. 'Puss, puss. Come on, Ginger,' she coaxed, but the cat refused to emerge.

'It's not coming,' said Tash.

'Maybe if we leave the door open, he'll come back in by himself?' suggested Clancy.

'I'm not standing here all day!'

'What about the poor cat? What if it gets run over?'

Tash shrugged. 'You can stay here and wait for the stupid cat if you want to. I'm going to see Pa.'

'Tash!' wailed Clancy, but her sister had already whisked herself inside.

Clancy stood for a few moments in the doorway, half in and half out, feeling the cool air-conditioning on her sweaty skin. She glanced nervously at the reception desk, but the chair behind it was empty. The receptionist must have been taking a lunch break. There was no movement from the cat.

At last Clancy cast a despairing glance around the foyer, grabbed a chair and propped it in position to hold the doors open in case Ginger changed his mind, then ran after Tash.

★ ★ ★

They found Pa in the big lounge room with the other residents. He was sitting in his wheelchair in front of the television, with his head drooping onto his chest. He seemed to be dozing, not watching the ancient movie that was playing on the screen.

'Whatcha watching, Pa?' Tash swooped in with a quick hug and a kiss. 'Is it *The Great Escape* again?'

Pa blinked at her in confusion, and shrugged. When he saw Clancy, he pulled a surprised face, and reached out his left hand to give hers a squeeze. His right hand lay unmoving in his lap. Since his stroke, he hadn't been able to use his right arm or hand, and he couldn't speak, at least not much. He could say *yes* and *no* and *bugger*, and that was about it. And although he could stand up on his right leg, it wasn't much use for walking.

A tiny wrinkled lady in the next chair gave a fretful groan.

'Bye, Myrna!' said Tash cheerfully as she pulled Pa's wheelchair out of the semicircle. Clancy trailed behind as Tash pushed Pa down the corridor to his room. It was big enough for a bed and a cupboard, and he had his own bathroom, but the window looked out onto a dull view of a corner of the building, and Pa often kept the curtain shut.

'Sp-sp-sp?' Pa gestured to Clancy and Tash, eyebrows raised. He held up three fingers, then two.

'I don't understand, Pa,' said Clancy.

'Sp-sp-sp!' He held up his left hand in midair, and waved it in the general direction of – somewhere.

'Sorry, Pa,' said Tash. 'I don't get it either.'

He thumped his fist on the arm of his chair. 'Sp-sp-sp!' He pointed to the group of family photos on the wall beside the bed. Tash scrambled up, pointing to one picture, then the next.

'No,' said Pa. 'No...' Then, triumphantly, 'Yes!'

It was a photograph of all of Pa and Nan's children as teenagers: Mark with a broad grin and crazy hair; Tim all spotty and sulky, hiding behind a floppy fringe; Polly, hair neatly combed with a worried expression on her face; and the identical twins, Pip and Bee, much younger than the others, long dark curls tumbling over their shoulders.

Clancy recognised them vaguely, but apart from Polly, she hadn't met most of them for years. After Nan died and Pa had gone to live at The Elms, the siblings had drifted in all directions and hardly saw each other anymore.

Tash took the photo down and Pa put his finger on Polly's face. 'Sp-sp?'

'Where's Polly?' guessed Tash. 'Why didn't she come this morning?'

'She's gone to Sydney,' said Clancy. 'Didn't she tell you?'

Tash frowned. 'It's supposed to be a secret.'

'Even from Pa? It's not like he can tell anyone.' Clancy perched gingerly on the edge of the bed. She felt slightly better now that another adult knew about Polly abandoning them, even if the adult was only Pa. Tash and Polly had agreed there was no need to worry Tim and Harriet by telling them about her little trip. 'You'll only be alone for one night,' said Polly. 'Two at the most. What could possibly happen in a couple of nights?'

'Absolutely nothing,' Tash assured her.

Clancy supposed they were right. Probably. And Pa didn't seem too worried. But Pa didn't know about Mark being arrested in New Zealand. Tim and Harriet and Polly had all agreed it would just upset him. It wasn't as if he could do anything to help. Polly had told him Tash and Clancy were staying with her just for fun. No wonder he was confused.

Clancy swung her legs back and forth and tried to think of something to talk about. Conversation with Pa was hard work, because it was so difficult for him to talk back.

'Want to look at photos?' Tash reached into a box at the top of the cupboard and pulled out an album. Clancy knelt on the bed so she could peer over Pa's shoulder while Tash turned the pages.

'There's your old house, at Rosella. Remember when me and Clancy were little and we all lived with you there, and you and Nan used to look after us while Mum and Dad were working?'

'Yes.' Pa smiled.

'No,' said Clancy sadly. She'd been too young; she could hardly remember the Rosella years at all. The family had lived with Nan and Pa until Clancy turned three and Bruno was born, when they'd moved to the apartment. But they'd still visited Rosella often, and always had Christmas there, though Harriet's family were upset about that. Rosella had sometimes felt more like home than their actual home did.

But now the house was rented out to pay for Pa's room at The Elms, and they couldn't even visit anymore.

'Look at me! How cute was I?' Tash studied a photo of her younger self with satisfaction.

'Sp-sp-sp.' Pa tapped the picture with one finger.

'Yes, that was my first footy,' agreed Tash.

'I was just as cute as you,' muttered Clancy, eyeing

a photo of herself in a high chair, with something that looked like pumpkin on her chin.

Pa turned a page and sighed as he stared at photos of his garden. It had almost been a wilderness, a bush garden, to attract the birds that he and Nan had watched from the deck.

'Is that Nan?' said Clancy, and for a moment they all paused silently to gaze at the photo of Nan at the beach, laughing and holding onto a big sunhat that framed her round face like a halo. There weren't many photos of Nan, because she had usually been the one behind the camera. Clancy found that the tighter she tried to hold onto her memories of Nan, the blurrier they became.

'Sp-sp-sp.' Pa touched Nan's laughing face gently with his finger.

Clancy picked up the album and some loose photographs fell out. 'What are these?'

They were strange photos, wheels of light above a dark horizon. 'Sp-sp!' explained Pa, gesturing upward. He mimed clicking a camera, and waggled his fingers.

'Did Nan take these?' asked Tash.

'Yes!'

'They look like those paintings. You know, that guy—' said Clancy. 'That Vincent guy?'

'Sp-sp-sp!' said Pa, excited.

'I know what they are!' said Tash. 'Star trails! Time lapse star photos. Is that it, Pa? Is that what Nan was doing?'

'Sp-sp-sp!' Pa launched into a long story, none of which the girls could understand. Seeing their blank faces, he banged his fist on the arm of his chair and let out a roar of frustration. He hit his forehead with his hand. 'Aargh!'

'Don't, Pa, don't!' begged Clancy.

Pa slumped in his chair. 'Sp-sp-sp,' he said gloomily. *Never mind.*

There was a short, bleak silence.

Tash changed the subject. 'Hey Pa, do you remember the day we moved out, and I went missing, and no one could find me? Everyone was freaking out. Mum crawled under the deck looking for me, Dad went up on the roof, Nan knocked on all the neighbours' doors, Bruno was screaming in the pram, Clancy was bawling—'

'I was not!' said Clancy.

'Yes, you were. You don't remember,' said Tash dismissively. 'But Pa, you ignored everyone else, and you went down the road to that patch of forest that joins onto the national park, and you found me there hiding under the trees. And I said I didn't want to move into the flat, and you and I should live in a cubby in the forest forever, just the two of us. Remember that?'

'Ah . . .' Pa nodded. But Clancy thought he didn't look too sure.

Tash slammed the album shut. 'What about a game of chess?' She rummaged in the cupboard. 'Memory? Snap? Monopoly?'

'*Not* Monopoly,' said Clancy.

'Sp-sp-sp?' asked Pa.

'Because she's a nightmare to play with!' Clancy glared at Tash. 'She steals all the one-dollar notes, so no one ever has the right change to pay rent, and she always builds hotels on the Jail and you're *not allowed to*.'

'That's what developers do in the real world. Get over it,' said Tash. 'I'm not as bad as Bruno. He buys one property of every colour to make a rainbow, and then no one can win. Want to play, Pa?'

Pa waved his hand wearily. 'Nah.'

'It's no fun with only two,' said Clancy.

'At least with two, you always get a winner.' But Tash put the box back on the shelf. 'I guess we'd better go,' she said. 'Lunch time.'

Clancy slid off the bed in relief. 'Is it lunch time for you, too, Pa?'

'Pfft!' Pa fired up briefly, tapping his watch indignantly. 'Sp-sp-sp!'

'Pa's had his already,' said Tash. 'They have lunch at twelve, and dinner at five, don't you, Pa?'

'Sp-sp-sp,' agreed Pa disgustedly.

Tash grabbed the handles of the wheelchair. 'Come on. If you're lucky, you might catch the end of *The Great Escape*.'

5

Clancy and Tash left their grandfather parked in front of the television. The movie had finished, and now there was a concert playing, with a violinist in a flamboyant cravat and a sparkling waistcoat. Pa snorted, but he seemed resigned to enduring it.

At the front door, they found pandemonium.

Half a dozen residents who were not supposed to leave the building had discovered the open door and taken their chance to shuffle through it. Now they had scattered along the street, or trundled across the road, as fast as their shaky legs and walking frames could take them.

Blue-uniformed staff were frantically sprinting out the door to bring them back, and the foyer swarmed with staff and residents and visitors, all talking excitedly. An announcement from the agitated receptionist echoed through the corridors: 'Staff to the front door. Code purple, repeat, we have a code purple!'

'Oh, Clancy.' Tash shook her head sorrowfully. 'What have you done?'

Clancy was struck silent with horror.

'But there's a *sign* on the *door*!' The manager of The Elms, a youngish white woman in a red jacket and unsteady high-heeled shoes, wobbled across the foyer. Her name tag read *Belinda*. 'Who is responsible for this?'

Clancy's face glowed hot with guilt and embarrassment. 'I'm really sorry,' she whispered. 'I didn't mean to. It was for the cat.'

Belinda wheeled around sharply. 'For the *cat*?'

Miserably, Clancy scuffed the toe of her shoe on the tiled floor. 'He ran out,' she mumbled. She wished Tash would say something. Tash was so much better at talking to people.

'What cat? There is no cat.' Belinda frowned. 'Are you visiting someone?'

'Yes, Pa – I mean, Godfrey Sanderson. He's our grandfather.'

'Godfrey is your grandfather?'

Belinda blinked. Clancy could guess why. Their mother was Chinese, but Pa wasn't – he was Tim's father. Tash and Clancy didn't look anything like Pa. Belinda's reaction was the kind of thing that made Tash furious, but it just made Clancy feel sort of tired.

Belinda recovered quickly. 'Didn't you see the sign on the door? *Do Not Allow Residents To Walk Out Unaccompanied*? Or did you think it would be funny? Is this some kind of prank?'

'*No!* The cat—' But clearly Belinda didn't believe in the cat. Clancy said miserably, 'I just didn't realise—'

'So if Godfrey is your grandpa, your mum is Polly, is she?'

'No, she's our aunt,' said Tash.

'I see.' Belinda turned to the receptionist. 'Lorraine, could you look up Polly Sanderson's number for me?' She swung back to the girls. 'Your aunt knows you're here, yeah? Maybe she'd better come and pick you up, and I can have a word to her about not letting children wander around without adult supervision. Don't you know how dangerous that is?'

Tash's eyes narrowed. 'We're not *children*. I can learn to drive next year.'

'Please don't call Polly,' begged Clancy. 'I'm really, really sorry. It'll never happen again, I promise.' *Because I am never, never coming back here as long as I live.* Everyone was staring at her. She wished a black hole would swallow her up.

'You can call Polly if you want, but she won't pick up,' said Tash coolly. 'She switches her phone off when she's at work.'

Those were both true statements, thought Clancy. And Tash hadn't actually said that Polly was at work *today*.

Belinda raised her thinly plucked eyebrows. 'Let's make sure. Lorraine?'

'Just checking,' said Lorraine hastily, tapping at her computer keyboard.

But before she could find Polly's number, there was an interruption.

'Sp-sp-sp?'

Clancy spun to see Pa in his wheelchair, rolled into the foyer by one of the staff, a cheerful-looking young African woman whose name tag read *Neneh*.

Pa waved his hand at the chaos in the foyer, the residents milling in confusion, staff rushing in and out. 'Sp-sp-sp?'

'There was a breakout,' Tash told him. 'Kind of *slightly* our fault.'

Clancy could have hugged her for using the word *our*.

Neneh shook her head at Pa. 'Oh, Goffrey, you in trouble again? Belinda throw you out this time for sure!'

Clancy gasped.

'She can't do that!' cried Tash. 'It had nothing to do with Pa!'

'I will be speaking to your daughter,' said Belinda to Pa. 'I can't let this pass without consequences.'

Pa gave an indignant, wordless roar.

'Pa doesn't want to stay in your stupid home anyway!' Tash's black eyes blazed, her chin jerked up, and in the next instant, she'd grabbed the handles of Pa's wheelchair and thrust him toward the doors. One of the staff was just guiding Myrna back inside with his hand on her walking frame. Tash shouted, 'Clancy! Door!'

Instinctively, Clancy sprang to obey. She heard Neneh burst out laughing, and Belinda shout, 'Wait a minute!'

But it was too late. Pa and Tash were already halfway down the drive. Clancy sprinted after them, and the doors hissed shut behind her.

6

'What are you going to do now?' panted Clancy. She had to jog to keep pace with Tash, who was marching Pa swiftly along the pavement, her face flushed with rage.

'Dunno,' said Tash shortly. And she muttered something that sounded vaguely swear-ish.

Clancy glanced over her shoulder. 'Tash! Someone's coming!'

'What are they going to do? Arrest us?'

'You shouldn't have taken Pa. That's kidnapping!'

'It's not kidnapping when the person wants to come with you.'

'Sp-sp-sp,' agreed Pa.

'Wait! Wait!' called the person thumping heavily along the footpath toward them.

'It's one of the nurses,' said Clancy. 'The smiley one. Neneh.'

Neneh thudded up beside them, gasping for breath, but still smiling. 'Hoo! You go fast!' She clutched at her side. 'Hoo!'

'Sp-sp-sp,' said Pa firmly.

Tash folded her arms. 'We're not going back there.'

'No, no, you have some – time out, yeah?' Neneh beamed at them. 'Okay, Goffrey? Let Belinda calm down?'

'Sp-sp-sp!' said Pa indignantly.

Neneh laid a soothing hand on his shoulder. 'I know, I know. You have little quiet time, yeah? Stay tonight with Polly, maybe?' She thrust a folded string of small plastic packets into Tash's hands. 'Goffrey's pills. Tonight, next day, you come back. No rush, yeah?'

Tash pushed the pills into her pocket. 'Maybe.'

'When you ready.' Neneh stood with her hands on her hips, still huffing for breath. 'Maybe Belinda not let you come back at all!' She wagged her finger at Pa, kissed him on the cheek, gave them a cheery wave, and strolled back down the street toward The Elms.

'Huh.' Tash gripped the wheelchair handles and pushed, more slowly than before. Clancy wondered if she should offer to help, but wheeling Pa was hard work. He wasn't a big man, but he was surprisingly heavy. Tash was better at that kind of thing.

Clancy trotted behind them. 'That Neneh seems pretty nice,' she ventured.

Tash snorted. Clancy heard a strange, strangled sound coming from their grandfather.

'Pa? Are you okay?'

But it was all right. He was laughing.

'It's not funny,' warned Tash. But the scary, murderous

expression had faded from her face, and Clancy felt safe to walk beside her.

Pa's hand shot out toward a little bird perched on a twig in someone's front garden. 'Sp-sp-sp!'

'What's that?' asked Clancy politely. 'A sparrow?'

Pa clapped his hand to his forehead in disbelief at her ignorance. 'No!'

'A willie wagtail?' guessed Tash.

'Ha! Sp-sp-sp!'

'I'll Google it when we get back,' promised Clancy.

'Birds are everywhere, you know,' said Tash. 'Every part of the world.'

'What about Antarctica?'

'Penguins?' said Tash scornfully.

'Oh, yeah, of course.' Clancy flushed. 'But penguins don't count. They can't fly.'

'*What*?' said Pa.

'What's the point of a bird that can't fly?' Clancy protested.

'Emus say hi. Ostriches. Kiwis.'

'Yeah, well, they're pointless, too.'

'Really? All of them?'

'Okay, okay.' Why did Tash always have to be right about *everything*?

When they reached Polly's house, they remembered the front steps, which of course the wheelchair couldn't go up. The passage at the side of the house was too narrow to wheel Pa around to the back door.

'Bugger!' said Pa.

'We'll have to stay out here,' said Tash. She pushed the chair into the shade on the tiny square of artificial grass that was Polly's low-maintenance, perfect front lawn, and spread out the doona from Clancy's bed for the girls to sit on. They brought out rice crackers and orange juice and jam and bananas and instant noodles, and had a weird but satisfying picnic. Pa needed a little help peeling bananas and spreading jam, but he coped pretty well with one hand. Clancy was impressed, but she thought if she'd had four years of practice, she'd probably have learned to manage all right, too.

'Mrs Christie next door is watching us,' she whispered.

Tash spun round and poked out her tongue.

'Tash! Rude!'

'I don't care. She should mind her own business.'

Clancy borrowed Tash's phone to look up the mystery bird. Tim and Harriet had promised Clancy a phone of her own when she started high school. If her parents hadn't gone to New Zealand, maybe Tim would have bought it this week. Clancy did want a phone, but she wasn't looking forward to what a phone of her own represented: responsibility, independence. Danger.

'Don't get jam on my phone,' warned Tash.

Clancy hastily licked her fingers, and wiped Tash's garish yellow phone cover on the doona. 'It was a fantail,' she announced in triumph, and held up the screen to show Pa.

'It could have been anything,' said Tash.

'Sp-sp-sp!'

'No, I'm right. See, Pa agrees with me.'

'No, he agrees with *me*!'

The sisters glared at each other.

'I'm right,' muttered Clancy, determined not to let Tash have the last word this time. 'I saw its tail.'

'Pfft!' Tash rolled onto her stomach and plucked out blades of fake grass. 'This would be a nice day for bird-watching if there were any interesting birds round here.'

Mine was interesting! Clancy wanted to say; but she knew Tash would scoff, so instead she pointed to a grey bird sidling at the edge of the lawn, eyeing their spilled crumbs. 'There's one.'

'A *pigeon*,' said Tash with deep scorn. 'I'm talking about birdwatching with real birds, like the ones that live at Rosella.'

Clancy said, 'There were a ton of birds at Rosella, weren't there, Pa? Do you miss it?'

Pa let out a long breath, tapped his chest, waved his hand into the distance and laid his hand on his heart.

'Of course he misses it, peabrain.' Tash sat up. 'Would you like to go back and see your house, Pa?'

'Yes!' Pa cried, then whispered under his breath, 'Yes, yes.'

'It's a long way to push him,' said Clancy.

'I could call one of those, you know, maxi-taxis.' Tash scrambled to her feet, eyes gleaming. 'We've got the emergency money.'

Polly had left them fifty dollars, just in case.

Clancy looked at Tash. 'We couldn't go inside. The house is rented out. People live there.'

'I know. But we could look at the garden, we could walk around the streets. It would be something to do. Do you want to, Pa?'

Pa sat bolt upright in his chair. 'Yes!' he roared, and let out a stream of word-ish noises, which was the closest he could come to talking in sentences since his stroke. 'Sp-sp-sp!' he finished vehemently.

Clancy gave Tash a worried look. 'Are we allowed to? Do you have to be over eighteen to order a taxi?'

Tash was already searching for a number on her phone. 'Anyone can order a taxi, if you can pay for it.' She held the phone to her ear. 'Hello? Can I book a taxi, please?'

Clancy gasped. Pa was smiling. Tash gave Polly's address, and the address of Pa's old house in Rosella. 'Okay, thanks.' She hung up. 'It'll be here in an hour.'

'We're really going? Seriously?'

Clancy was half excited, half terrified. If she'd known how far they would end up travelling before the weekend was over, she wouldn't have wasted her energies being frightened of a taxi trip to Rosella.

'Of course we're going. Why not? Clancy, you've got to stop being scared of everything.'

'I'm not,' muttered Clancy furiously.

Tash opened her mouth to argue, but at that moment

Pa waved at her and indicated that he needed to use the toilet.

Clancy leapt up. 'What will we do? Will we have to take him back to The Elms?'

'Oh my God, Clancy, this is exactly what I'm talking about! Don't be so pathetic! It's no big deal. I can handle it. I've done it at The Elms before.'

'No way, gross!' cried Clancy, before she could stop herself.

'It's easy. If he only has to use a bottle, he can do it all himself. Otherwise, he just needs a hand getting on and off the seat and back into the wheelchair.' Tash leaned closer to whisper, 'And he wears a pull-up, just in case.'

'You mean – a *nappy*?'

'Just in case of accidents. It's not like he ever actually needs it.'

'Sp-sp-sp!' called Pa urgently, and Tash hurried over.

By the time she had wheeled Pa into the garage so that Mrs Christie couldn't see what was going on, and Clancy had gulped down the last of the orange juice so Pa could pee into the bottle, and Tash had taken the bottle away and disposed of the wee while Pa hitched up his tracksuit pants, and they'd rolled outside again, and everyone had washed their hands, or in Pa's case, used Polly's antiseptic wipes, Tash had completely forgotten that she'd been in the middle of telling Clancy how hopeless she was.

Clancy decided not to remind her.

The big yellow taxi took more than an hour to arrive, but Clancy thought it was worth the wait – firstly because it was from Comet Taxis, which was a most excellent name, and secondly because the driver was spectacular.

He was called Sidhu, and he wore a turban and shoes with long pointed toes, and a luscious black moustache. Sidhu had a big cheerful laugh, and he was making Pa's wish to go home come true. If Sidhu could grant a wish for Pa, maybe he could organise a couple of wishes for Clancy, too?

It probably wasn't polite to ask for wishes from someone you'd only just met. Safer to wish upon a star instead, decided Clancy; or a comet.

If she could wish upon a star and have that wish come true, what would she wish for? To make her first year at high school go well? To be as bold and brave and smart and popular as Tash? She'd never be able to tell Tash that wish.

Maybe it was better to wish that she didn't have to start high school at all. She could wish that nothing ever had to change. Then she'd never have anything to feel scared of. An end to entropy – that's what she should wish for!

Although altering the fundamental laws of the universe was a pretty big wish for a single star to handle...

'Clancy! Are you coming or what?'

'Coming,' said Clancy hastily.

The driver let down a platform at the back of the van and pushed Pa's chair onto it, then the platform lifted up so the wheelchair rolled straight inside. Sidhu showed Tash how to fasten the web of hooks and straps and buckles that held Pa and the chair firmly in place.

'You have the card?' asked Sidhu. 'The taxi card? For claiming your discount?'

Clancy and Tash didn't know what the taxi driver was talking about. Pa knew, but he couldn't make Tash understand, and in the end they just gave up. Much later they found out that Polly had a special government card that meant that Pa only had to pay half-fare for a maxi-taxi.

'O-*kay*!' cried Sidhu, when they were all buckled into their seats. The Comet taxi purred like a lion and drew away from the kerb, and they were on their way.

'Ha-ha!' cried Pa, beaming, and he clutched at Tash's hand, which was his way of saying *thank you*.

Tash could be super annoying, thought Clancy; but she had to admit that her sister made things happen.

The big yellow taxi trundled out of Tutt's Flat and up into the hills, along the highway and past the shops, under the railway bridge and past the entrance to the national park, then turned off the main road and into a maze of short, steep streets.

Clancy could vaguely remember some landmarks, like the fire station, and the red house on the corner. But Tash was confidently calling out directions to Sidhu – 'Left here. Next right.' – even though he had a GPS and paid no attention to her, just laughed his big hearty laugh and sang out, 'O-*kay*!'

The drive took about twenty minutes. Clancy was facing forward, so she could see the meter ticking over, chewing into Polly's emergency fifty-dollar note. She wanted to warn Tash, who was facing backward, that this trip was going to use all their cash; but she told herself that it would only worry Pa, so she kept quiet. This was Tash's adventure, so looking after the money was Tash's responsibility, not Clancy's business. There had to be some advantages to being born second.

Pa peered intently through the windows with bright blue eyes. At last the taxi swung down a narrow street and Pa whispered, 'So-it-is!'

The sprawling brown-brick house that he and Nan had built, and where they'd raised their family, lay half-hidden inside a thicket of trees, much more wild and overgrown than Clancy remembered.

'What's that?' cried Tash sharply.

A large *For Sale* sign was standing by the letterbox.

'Sidhu, stop here!' Tash called, and she jumped out of the taxi and ran down the driveway for a closer look.

'Sp-sp-sp?' Pa twisted round to stare at the board.

'Did you know they were selling your house, Pa?' asked Clancy. 'Did Polly tell you?"

Pa shook his head. 'Nah, nah.' He pointed to Clancy and raised his eyebrows in a question.

'We didn't know either.' Clancy wrung her hands together. 'But it's your house! How could they?'

Tash ran back up the drive and called out, 'There's no one here! The house is empty! Can you drive down to the front door?'

'Sure, sure.' Sidhu backed the taxi carefully down the driveway's gentle slope.

Pa was silent as the platform lowered his wheel-chair onto the gravel, carpeted with dead leaves. Clancy grabbed the handles while Tash paid Sidhu with Polly's fifty-dollar note. He gave her back a twenty and then a five; so they'd have just enough to take Pa back to The Elms. Clancy let out a private sigh of relief.

'What time would you like me to return?' asked Sidhu, as if he'd read her mind.

'I'll call you,' said Tash grandly.

Sidhu's moustache drooped doubtfully. 'It can be a busy time, in the evening,' he warned; then he shrugged and smiled. 'O-*kay*!'

The taxi zoomed up the drive and left them standing there in the cool shade of the trees.

'I can't believe they're selling your *home*!' Tash burst out. 'Without telling you! That rat Polly didn't even *mention* it!'

'Dad must know, too,' said Clancy. 'And he didn't say anything either.'

'Yeah, well, that is deeply disappointing. He's a rat, too.'

'Sp-sp-sp.' Pa hunched over in his chair, his face suddenly old and sad.

Clancy hovered uncertainly behind Pa's shoulder while Tash cupped her hands to peer through a window. 'Definitely no one here,' she reported. 'How cool would it be if we could get inside?'

Suddenly Pa straightened his back. 'Sp-sp-sp!' He mimed inserting a key into a lock and opening a door.

'Yes, but we don't have the key, Pa,' said Clancy.

'Ah!' Pa tapped the side of his nose, and a mischievous expression lit up his face. 'Sp-sp-sp!'

'What, you've got a key?' said Tash. 'In your pocket?'

'Pfft!' *Don't be silly.* Pa gestured for Clancy to push him to the side of the house.

'I can't take you down that path, Pa. It's too steep,' said Clancy in alarm. 'We'd crash!'

Pa gave an exaggerated, exasperated sigh, and jabbed his finger in the same direction.

'Down there?' said Tash. 'Something around there? The back door? The deck?'

'Under the house?' guessed Clancy, and Pa swung round in excitement.

'Yes!' He mimed opening a door, and groping above his head. He held up a small invisible object. 'Aha!'

Without another word, Tash leapt down the path by the side of the house. Clancy heard a bang as her sister threw open the little door and vanished inside, then some muffled swearing.

'Sp-sp-sp!' Pa urged Clancy.

'You think I should go and help her?' Clancy hung back. She'd always been scared of the dark, dank, creepy cavity beneath the house. 'I think someone should stay here with you.'

'Pfft!' Pa reached down and firmly applied his brake. 'Sp-sp!' He waved her on her way, and reluctantly Clancy edged down the path. She reached the door just in time to meet Tash as she emerged, brushing cobwebs from her hair.

'So many, many spiders,' announced Tash. 'And I can't find it.'

'Didn't Pa say it was above the door?'

'You have a look.'

Clancy hung back. 'But – spiders!'

Tash groaned theatrically and disappeared back under the house. There was more swearing, less muffled this time, and then a howl of triumph. 'Got it!'

Tash sprinted up the path, brandishing an old, dirt-encrusted brass key attached to a miniature model of the Eiffel Tower. 'Is this it, Pa?'

Pa examined the key and the key ring. 'Yes.'

'Wow,' said Clancy. 'How many years has that been there?'

Pa held up five fingers, flashed five again, five again, looked slightly lost, and shrugged.

'A long time, anyway,' said Clancy.

'Moment of truth. Are you excited?' Tash wiggled the key into the front door lock, paused for dramatic effect, and grinned at Pa. 'It's open!'

'Tash, do you think we should…?' began Clancy nervously, but Tash talked over her.

'Hey, we could stay here for dinner! We could get pizza delivered!'

There was a short pause. Clancy said cautiously, 'If we *did* get pizza – hypothetically – would we have enough money for the taxi back?'

'Sure,' said Tash after a moment. 'I think so.'

'I don't think we would,' said Clancy.

The sisters stared at each other.

'Sp-sp-sp?' said Pa.

'Oh, nothing. It's just Clancy always has to ruin everything,' said Tash bitterly. 'Because she's a *ruiner*.'

'Sp-sp?'

'She thinks we're going to run out of cash!'

As if that was a totally ridiculous idea, instead of a *rational*, *reasonable* thing to worry about, thought Clancy crossly.

Pa gave a sudden gasp, as if he'd had an electric shock. 'Hah!' He jabbed his finger urgently back at the side of the house. 'Sp-sp-sp!'

'What?' Tash frowned. 'You don't want to go inside? You want to go round the back?'

Pa shook his head impatiently. 'Yeah – no!'

'Do you need the toilet again?' asked Clancy.

'There's something else under the house?' guessed Tash. 'A secret tunnel? A trapdoor?'

'Pfft!' Pa held up his finger. He mimed pushing his way through a jungle, or a curtain, peering into darkness, then grasping something in his hand. 'Aha!'

'But I found the key already.' Tash pushed the front door open and sighed. 'I'll go and look. Clancy, ruiner, you take Pa inside.'

'But Tash, are you sure we're allowed? Is this legal?'

Furiously Tash grabbed the wheelchair handles. 'Okay, I'll take Pa in, and *you* go and look.'

'Tash, don't be mean!' wailed Clancy, as if she and Tash were still six and eight, instead of twelve (about to start high school) and fourteen (playing in a football team with adult women, and able to learn to drive next year). But Tash had already trundled Pa inside.

8

She can't make me.

But somehow, an ancient force of obedience to her older sister drove Clancy down the path to the little wooden door. The dugout under the house was like a cave, where Pa had kept his chainsaw and ladders; but the tenants had asked Polly for a proper garden shed instead. Maybe they didn't like spiders either. Shuddering, her hands held out protectively in front of her, Clancy shuffled into the darkness.

She stood there, blinking, while her eyes adjusted. Tiny stars of light shone through the ventilation grilles, and soon Clancy found that she could see veils of cobwebs strung across the low-roofed cavity.

'I'm not going any further in!' she said aloud.

Stepping back, she heard a crunch and her heart jumped as her foot came down on something – a snake? A rat trap? No, it was just a long stick. Instinctively she picked it up like a sword and slashed it back and forth until most of the cobwebs were gone. Tash had had it easy, with the key above the door. Whatever the other thing was that Pa wanted, it was obviously hidden right at the back of the dugout. Maybe it was even buried. How would she ever find it?

A sudden memory returned to Clancy, from when she was very little. She remembered coming down here with Nan, and her grandmother holding her hand. *The dark is nothing to be scared of*, Nan had said; *without the dark, we wouldn't have the stars*. And with Nan's hand gripping hers, Clancy hadn't been quite so scared to go under the house.

The memory was so vivid that Clancy even caught a whiff of the lily-of-the-valley perfume that Nan had always worn, as if her grandmother were standing right beside her.

'Nan?' whispered Clancy. She inched forward, her sword-stick raised in front of her. The ladders and boxes and chainsaws Pa had stored down here had been cleared out before the house was rented. Polly had probably already found whatever it was Pa had hidden...although she hadn't discovered that spare key.

Come on, Clancy. Nothing to be scared of.

Narrow rods of sunlight poked through the grilles as she edged forward. Was that something moving in the shadows? Clancy whirled around, but the space was empty – there was nowhere to hide. She crept right up to the earth wall at the very back of the dugout and touched it with her fingertips. And there was the scent of lily-of-the-valley again, just for a split second, stronger this time in the stale air.

'Nan? Am I getting warmer?'

Clancy tapped the wall with her stick, then she ran it along the top of the wall where the cavity joined the underside of the house.

The tip of the stick struck something. Something metallic, something hard.

Clancy's heart bumped. She stretched up on her toes and swept the stick across the rough ledge at the top of the wall. A rusted old biscuit tin jumped out and clattered at her feet.

For a second she stood there frozen, disbelieving. Then she picked up the tin and hugged it to her chest as she stumbled to the doorway. Sunlight blinded her as she ran up the path to the front door, and burst into the house.

'Is this it, Pa? Is this what you were talking about?'

Pa was in his wheelchair in front of the big glass doors that opened onto the deck. Tash was just pulling back the curtains so he could see the view.

Clancy dropped the tin in his lap and Pa gave a shout of delight. He struggled to prise off the lid with one hand, but he couldn't manage it, even with Clancy holding onto the tin.

'What's that?' Tash took the tin and yanked off the rusted lid.

Crumpled orange and purple and blue banknotes fluttered to the floor like a cloud of butterflies.

'Aha!' cried Pa. 'Sp-sp-sp!' He launched into one of his long, incomprehensible stories, with many gestures and much arm-waving. But he seemed to realise quickly that it was hopeless this time, and shrugged his shoulder to say, *well, there it is, anyway.*

'So you hid the money under the house?' said Clancy. 'What for?'

'Sp-sp-sp,' explained Pa.

Tash knelt down and began gathering the notes into piles. 'There's about five hundred dollars here! Did you rob a bank? Was it in case the house burned down in a bushfire? Or were you hiding it from the tax office?'

'Sp-sp-sp!' said Pa indignantly.

'And Polly doesn't know about this?' asked Clancy, thrilled. 'Or Dad, or Mark, or the twins?'

'Nope,' said Pa smugly.

'Did Nan know?'

Pa's face softened. 'Yes.'

Clancy almost told them then, about the scent of lily-of-the-valley, and that sudden vivid memory that had pushed her forward. But she knew Tash wouldn't believe her. She wasn't sure she believed it herself. Instead she said vaguely, 'Maybe Nan helped me find it. Maybe she was, I dunno, guiding me.'

'Lucky she didn't guide the tenants.' Tash sat back on her heels. 'Well, we are definitely getting pizza now.'

It was strange being in Pa's empty house, with no furniture, no books on the shelves, and none of Nan's photographs on the walls. The echoing rooms felt bigger than Clancy remembered. The house was cool and dim and shadowy, with the musty smell that rooms acquire when they've been closed up for a while.

Pa didn't seem very interested in the house itself. He was gazing out at the view of the national park, the slopes blanketed with deep grey-green, and the huge, overgrown garden with its towering gum trees.

'Sp-sp-sp!' He gestured impatiently and Tash pushed him out onto the deck.

Nan and Pa's house had been built on a double block, more like a patch of bushland than a garden, except for the section near the deck where he'd tended his vegetable beds and fruit trees. A cockatoo screamed from the top of a massive eucalypt, then swooped over the roof with sunlight dazzling on its bright white wings.

'Sp-sp-sp!'

'Even I don't need to look up that one,' said Clancy.

Pa clucked his tongue as he noticed the dandelions and wild onion grass that had sprung up in the vegetable patch, and the rotting, fallen fruit beneath the lemon and orange trees. 'Sp-sp-sp,' he said gloomily.

Tash leaned precariously over the railing. 'But check out the apples, Pa.'

The apple tree was laden with golden fruit like Christmas baubles. 'Ha!' said Pa, pleased. 'So-it-is.'

Tash gave him a teasing nudge. 'They grew all by themselves, without any help from you!'

'Nah!' protested Pa. 'Sp-sp-sp.'

Tash ran down the steps from the deck and picked an armful of apples. She and Pa and Clancy sat out on the deck as the golden sunshine slanted through the trees, crunching and slurping. The apples were sweet and crisp and juicy. Far away, a kookaburra let out a joyous laugh, and Clancy forgot to be worried about being there. If her grandmother's ghost was haunting the house, she thought, Nan would be glad to see them sitting here together, eating apples, just like when she was still alive and Clancy's family had lived there with her and Pa. Clancy had eaten apples then, too. Nan had cut them up for her. She was sure she could remember that. Clancy took another bite.

While they waited for Pa to finish in the toilet, Tash propped herself against the wall as she scrolled through her phone.

'Streaks?' said Clancy.

'Ordering pizza.'

'Oh! Were you serious about that?'

'Of course. Why not?'

'But – shouldn't we take Pa home soon? Won't they be worried?'

'They're not expecting him at The Elms. That nurse said we should keep him overnight at Polly's, remember? And I've got his pills. Anyway,' added Tash, 'Pa *is* home.'

Clancy scuffed the carpet with her toe and said nothing.

'Come on, Clance!' hissed Tash. 'Don't ruin this as well. Pa's so happy. We can't take him back to that horrible place. He'd much rather be here.'

'You always think you can read Pa's mind!' whispered Clancy fiercely. 'But you don't know what he's thinking.'

Pa banged on the wall to say he was ready to come out. Tash wheeled the chair into the bathroom and helped him shuffle round and drop into the seat. 'You don't want to leave yet, do you, Pa? You want to stay a bit longer?'

Pa laid his hand on his heart, gazed at the ceiling and murmured. He gestured all around, then pressed his hand to his heart again.

Tash gave Clancy a look. 'I'm taking that as a yes.'

Clancy sighed. 'Okay, okay.'

They took Pa on a tour of the empty house while they waited for the pizza to arrive: the yellow master bedroom, Mark and Tim's blue room, the green-painted room that had once been Polly's, the pink bedroom that the twins had shared. The old-fashioned bathroom had a deep tub that Tash and Clancy and Bruno had all fitted in together on weekend visits. (Tash shuddered. 'Thank God Nan never took a photo of *that*!')

There was a built-in cupboard tucked into a corner of the dining room where Clancy used to hide (she could hardly squeeze into it now) and a broad window seat where Nan used to sit and read.

'And she had a telescope out on the deck, didn't she?' said Tash. 'I wonder what happened to that?'

'Sp-sp-sp,' said Pa; but of course they didn't understand.

'Nan had a telescope?' said Clancy. 'Is that where I get it from?'

'Clancy has this thing about space,' Tash told Pa.

'Ah!' Pa pointed up to the roof, then made a circle with his fingers and mimed peering through it. 'Hm.' He looked expectantly up at Clancy.

'Nan liked stars, too?' said Tash. 'Is that what you're saying, Pa?'

'Yes, yes!'

Pa fumbled for Clancy's hand and squeezed it.

If only Nan hadn't died, thought Clancy sadly. They could have talked about astronomy. Nan could have taught her how to use a telescope and they could have watched the stars together. Maybe she and Nan would have become special friends, the way that Pa and Tash were. Maybe

Clancy would have been Nan's favourite grandchild, the way Bruno was the favourite of Po Po, their Chinese grandmother in Sydney. But now she'd never know.

Holding hands, she and Pa gazed out of the window in silence.

10

By the time they'd eaten the pizza, twilight was creeping over the hills, and Clancy was fidgety.

'Tash? Are you going to call the taxi now?'

Tash looked across at Pa. 'You don't want to go back to The Elms yet, do you?'

The light went out of Pa's eyes, and his head drooped. 'No,' he whispered, so softly that Clancy barely heard him.

Tash put her arm around his shoulders. 'We could stay a bit longer.'

Clancy stared at her. 'Stay? You mean, stay here?'

'Why not? No one will even know. The staff at The Elms think he's at Polly's, they won't care.'

'But—'

'Pfft!' Pa walked his fingers through the air, flicked them, shielded his eyes to scan the horizon, and gave an exaggerated shrug.

'Even if they did know he was here, they wouldn't care,' translated Tash. 'They don't even want him back. You heard what that nurse said – he's always in trouble.'

'Sp-sp,' agreed Pa.

'Neneh,' murmured Clancy.

'What?'

'That nurse – her name's Neneh.'

'Whatever,' said Tash irritably.

There was a short silence.

Clancy said, 'But there's no furniture. Where are we going to sleep?'

'Curtains,' said Tash matter-of-factly. 'And Pa can sleep in his chair. He sleeps in his chair all day at The Elms.'

'Sp-sp,' said Pa. *Watch this*. Awkwardly, one-handed, he wheeled himself across to the window seat and raised his left foot to rest it on the ledge. 'Ta-da!'

'See?' said Tash. 'He'll be fine.'

'Ah!' Pa pointed to his open mouth.

'Are you still hungry? Do you want more pizza? A drink?'

Pa shook his head.

'Medicine?' guessed Clancy.

'Yes!' Pa beamed at her.

Tash clicked her fingers. 'Good call, peanut.'

Clancy glowed with pride.

They filled a water bottle for Pa, and Tash poured the evening's allocation of pills into his palm. 'Seven – *eight*! What are they all for?'

Pa shrugged stoically as he swallowed them all down.

'Wow,' said Clancy, who would rather suffer a head-ache than force herself to choke down a painkiller. 'That is a lot of pills.'

Tash unhooked the bedroom curtains and Pa propped his feet on the window seat, cuddled himself under folds of drapery and gave the girls a thumbs-up. He was so tired that he fell asleep almost instantly.

'They put them to bed at six-thirty at The Elms,' said Tash.

It was nearly dark outside. Clancy slipped out onto the deck to gaze up at the sky. The full moon was pasted above the black bulk of the hills like a disc of silver foil. The trees blocked out some sections of the sky, but there was a clear patch where Clancy could see a scattering of stars. They were much sharper than the stars she could make out through the window at home, and there were more of them. If only she had Nan's telescope, she might have been able to find some planets, she might have been able to read the January stars...

Nan? thought Clancy experimentally. *Are you here?* She sniffed tentatively, but she couldn't detect any lily-of-the-valley.

And then a point of light streaked across the sky, plunged behind the hills and vanished.

It was so fast that Clancy wasn't certain she'd really seen it. But her heart was pounding hard, and she knew, she *knew*, it was a sign from her grandmother.

She jumped as the sliding door behind her rasped and Tash came out onto the deck. 'What are you doing out here? I've made us beds out of curtains. Come and look.'

'I saw a meteor, Tash! I asked Nan for a sign, and then there was a meteor! She's here, she's watching us!'

'Yeah, right. Nan's ghost can set off shooting stars. I thought you believed in science?'

'I do – I know – but still . . . Can you smell that?'

'All I can smell is gum trees and your sweaty socks. Why, what can you smell?'

'Nothing,' said Clancy. 'It's gone now.'

Tash folded her arms and squinted at the sky. 'Hey, Nan! Are you listening? Send us another meteorite.'

'It's a meteor when it's in the atmosphere,' said Clancy. 'It's only a meteorite when it hits the ground.'

Tash flourished her arm. 'Whatever it is, I'm not seeing it. Or smelling it.'

Maybe she did it for me because I'm her favourite, thought Clancy. But she didn't say so.

'Go on, make her do it again,' said Tash.

'Magic doesn't work like that,' said Clancy stubbornly.

'How convenient,' said Tash. 'Come inside.'

Tash had made nests for them both from the soft netting of the curtains. Clancy wriggled about. 'I wish I had a pillow.'

'Stop whingeing. This is heaps more comfortable than some places I've slept.' Tash was the veteran of spontaneous sleepovers at her friends' houses, and occasionally went camping with them. She even kept a toothbrush and deodorant in her bag, to be prepared.

Clancy, who was attached to the comfort of her own bed, said nothing. But even she had to admit that it was kind of exciting to be camped out on the living room floor of an empty house, with moonlight flooding in and birds chirruping sleepily in the trees outside. And she was nearly as tired as Pa. It had been a long day.

Tash leaned against the wall, thumbing a text to Tim and Harriet in New Zealand. 'Just getting in first...*All fine here, talk soon, love you, kiss kiss*.'

Clancy startled awake when Tash's phone buzzed. 'Mum and Dad?' she hissed.

'No, it's Polly.' Tash shoved the phone under a fold of curtain. 'I won't pick up. She'll think I'm out of juice. I nearly am, anyway.'

Clancy snuggled down again. Today had been fun, mostly, but she'd be relieved when Pa had been delivered safely back to The Elms. Hopefully no one would ever find out what they'd done...Hopefully Tash's phone battery would last till morning so they could call Comet Taxis for Sidhu to come and pick them up...

'Tash?' she whispered.

'Yo.'

'Are you sure this is okay? Us being here?'

'Of course! This is *Pa's house*.'

'I guess,' murmured Clancy doubtfully. Then she remembered that at least Nan seemed to approve. That was a comforting thought.

There was a rustling from the other side of the room as Tash wriggled out of her nest.

'What are you doing?' whispered Clancy.

'I forgot to put the security chain on the door.'

Clancy clutched the curtains under her chin. 'Do you think a gang of home invaders might break in?'

'Jeez, Clancy, no!' A pause. 'But Pa always did it before he went to bed. Remember?'

'How could I remember? I was always asleep.'

Tash laughed softly in the shadows. 'Fair point.'

'Tash?'

'What?'

'I just thought…nobody in the whole world knows where we are right now.'

'Hey, you're right. *Awesome*.' Tash's voice was sounding sleepy.

A longer pause.

'Tash?' whispered Clancy. 'If Nan could see us now, what do you think she'd say?'

'Shut up and go to sleep, probably…'

'What's funny?'

'I didn't laugh.'

'But I heard you.'

'Must have been Pa.'

'It didn't sound like Pa…'

Tash heaved herself over. 'Shut up, Clancy-Pants, I'm trying to sleep.'

'Are you *sure* you didn't laugh?' whispered Clancy after a moment.

But there was no reply.

Clancy's last thought before she fell asleep was that she wished she'd brought a toothbrush, too.

Clancy was dreaming.

In her dream, she was sleeping in the pink room that she and Tash had shared when the family lived at Rosella, the twins' old room, and Nan was bending over the bed, gently shaking her shoulder. *Clancy,* her grandmother whispered, *it's time to wake up now...*

Clancy woke with a jump.

It was morning, and the front door was rattling and thumping as someone tried to force their way inside.

'Tash!' squeaked Clancy.

But Tash was already up, creeping to the door like a ninja, the nest of curtains kicked aside. Pa was awake, blinking blearily around as if he'd forgotten where he was, his curtain-covering slithering to the floor. Clancy huddled beneath the fabric, her heart beating fast.

The stranger outside pushed the door impatiently, but the chain held. There was a brief silence, then the person put their mouth to the crack and called sharply, 'Is somebody in there?'

Clancy's eyes widened.

Tash stood close to the door, but out of sight. Boldly she called, 'Who's there?'

'Who are you?' demanded the woman outside.

'I asked first,' countered Tash.

The door shook violently. 'What are you doing here? This house is supposed to be vacant.'

Clancy crawled over to shelter behind her sister. 'Tash, do something!'

Tash yelled, 'This is our grandfather's house, and he's here with us!'

'Oh, really?' said the voice. 'It says here, the owner of the property is…' there was a brief pause '…a Ms Pauline Sanderson.'

Pa let out an indignant roar.

'She's our aunt!' called Tash. 'And she's not the owner, our grandfather is! He's right here!'

'Then perhaps I'd better speak to him.'

Tash screwed up her face. 'You can't, he's… asleep.'

'Sp-sp-sp!' protested Pa, struggling to lower his stiff legs from the window seat, and smoothing down his hair with one hand.

'Can you wake him up so we can sort this out?' The woman sounded sceptical. 'I'm the real estate agent, Melissa Katselas, from Whately and Robinson. I'm here to do the condition report, and you guys were supposed to be out of the house three days ago.'

'We're not the tenants!' shouted Tash. 'I keep trying to tell you – my grandfather owns this house.'

There was a short silence.

'I'm going to count to five,' called Melissa. 'And if this alleged grandfather of yours isn't out here to explain to me what you're doing, then I am calling the police and reporting a break-in.'

'Sp-sp-sp!' called Pa. 'N-n-n-nah!' He was trying to force out his words, but they wouldn't come.

'Tash!' Clancy hissed from the window. 'She's doing it, she's calling them!'

Tash fumbled with the chain and flung the door open. 'My grandfather can't talk to you,' she said desperately. 'He has aphasia.'

The woman swung round suspiciously. 'He has what?'

'Aphasia. He had a stroke, and now he can't speak anymore. He can say "yes" and "no" and "bugger", and sometimes other words sort of burst out, but only when he's not thinking about it, not when he tries to say them on purpose—'

'Never heard of it.' Melissa folded her arms.

She was thin, sharp-nosed and dressed in black pants and a leather jacket. Maybe she was a *secret* agent, thought Clancy, peering through the crack in the curtains. A spy – an assassin!

'What about your parents? Are they in there with you?'

'They're in New Zealand!' called Clancy.

'I'm calling Pauline,' announced Melissa, punching a number into her phone.

Clancy and Tash exchanged desperate glances. But after a moment Melissa removed the phone from her ear. 'Voicemail...'

Tash let out a sigh of relief.

'Let me talk to your grandfather,' said Melissa. 'If he's really here. Or else I *will* call the police.' She made a sudden lunge to get through the doorway, but Tash slammed the door shut and twisted the deadlock so that Melissa couldn't open it.

Clancy cried out in terror, 'Tash, we're going to be arrested!'

'No, we're not.' Tash was racing around the living room, pushing her feet into her runners, seizing the tin with Pa's stash of cash and shoving it into her backpack. She grabbed her phone and jammed it in on top. 'Here, Clance, you take this. Ready to go, Pa? Cos when I say *run*, we're going to run.'

12

Clancy was beside the door, struggling to zip up the overstuffed backpack. 'Chain!' commanded Tash in a whisper. Clancy gently eased the security chain from its groove with fingers that trembled, doing her best to be as quiet as possible. Tash stood by, gripping the handles of Pa's wheelchair. Outside, they could hear Melissa the (secret) agent saying, 'I don't *want* to call the police. I don't *want* to report you for breaking and entering, but if I have to...'

'Ready?' hissed Tash.

Clancy nodded.

'Go!' shouted Pa unexpectedly, and Clancy twisted the deadlock and threw the door open. She caught a glimpse of Melissa's shocked face as Tash pushed Pa's wheelchair at her like a battering ram and she leapt out of the way, and then they were surging up the drive, Tash's backpack bumping on Clancy's shoulder, Pa whooping with excitement as Tash grunted, head down, driving the wheelchair up the slope with all her strength.

Clancy heard Melissa howl, '—assaulting me! With a *wheelchair*!' but by then they were at the top of the driveway and Pa's chair was swerving down the street with Tash clutching the handles and Clancy sprinting behind them.

'Come on!' yelled Tash.

'Ah! Ah!' Pa shouted, but Clancy couldn't tell if he was alarmed or delighted.

'Are you going to call the taxi now?' yelled Clancy.

'No time!' Tash shouted back.

She swung the wheelchair round a corner and they ran down the next hill at top speed, Tash pulling back hard, barely keeping the chair under control. The air was cool and fresh, and the sun poured down the hillsides of the national park in a flood of liquid gold. Pa raised his left arm and waved it gleefully. 'Woooh!'

As they ran, Clancy heard the wail of a siren.

'Tash! She did call the police! They're coming!'

Without missing a beat, Tash swerved the chair off the road and onto the gravel track that led into the same dense patch of forest where she'd hidden as a little girl on moving day so many years ago. Clancy stumbled after her, tripping over the ruts in the path. The wheelchair bumped and rattled and Pa protested.

Clancy gasped as she noticed a rough carving on the trunk of a tall, slim gum tree: a five pointed star, and a crescent moon. 'Tash! This way!'

They ducked into a sheltered pocket, just off the path, where they could hide in the thick undergrowth. Clancy leaned against the tree, clutching a stitch in her side, her heart hammering. Tash peered out as the police car zoomed past, siren shrieking. Something bright yellow crunched under its wheels; fragments flew and clattered.

Tash whipped round. 'Where's my phone?'

Clancy gulped. 'In the bag…'

Tash snatched the backpack. 'You didn't zip it up!'

'I was trying – there wasn't time.'

Tash rummaged. 'My phone's not here.' She shoved the bag at Clancy and took off for the road, leaving Clancy to grab at the handles of Pa's chair and slowly, painfully, bump him back along the track.

Tash was squatting by the side of the road, silently collecting up the shattered remains of her phone.

'Bugger!' said Pa.

'It must have fallen out,' faltered Clancy. 'When we were running—'

'Oh, you think?' Tash shot her a fierce glare. 'Thanks, genius. And I've lost all my streaks…all my photos…my messages…everything!'

'I'm sorry,' whispered Clancy, stricken. 'I'm so, so sorry!'

Tash stood up abruptly, snapped her fingers for the pack and slung it onto her own back. Then she took the handles of Pa's wheelchair. Clearly Clancy was not fit to be trusted with responsibility for anything.

Before this disaster struck, Clancy had been going to tell Tash about the carving of the star and the moon on the tree, another clear sign from their grandmother. But obviously her sister wouldn't listen now.

Miserably Clancy followed Tash and Pa along the side of the road, bending to pick up shards of bright yellow plastic here and there. Better not to leave clues for the police to find, covered in Tash's fingerprints and DNA, pointing out their trail...

A thought struck her. 'I guess we can't ring for the taxi now.'

Tash didn't bother to reply, just shot a withering glance over her shoulder and marched on, pushing the wheelchair ahead of her in short, angry jerks.

If Clancy hadn't felt so guilty about the phone, and so jumpy about the possibility of the police car coming back, she might have enjoyed that walk. The smell of eucalyptus grew stronger as the air warmed, and cockatoos screeched gleefully from the depths of the forest. The moon still shone palely, low in the sky, a circle of tracing paper now rather than silver foil.

When the side street joined the main highway, Tash was able to tilt the wheelchair up onto the cracked concrete footpath instead of pushing it along the edge of the bitumen.

'Tash? Don't you think we're a bit...noticeable?'

'Oh, have you got an invisibility cloak you forgot to mention? This is the only road from here.'

Clancy lapsed back into silence. Obviously Tash wasn't over the loss of her phone yet. Considering how much Tash loved her phone, that could take years.

Nervously Clancy glanced back over her shoulder now and again as they trudged under the railway bridge and past the fire station, in case the police car reappeared; though if they hadn't shown up by now, they must have driven along the other road over the hill from Pa's place. Maybe Nan had nudged them that way somehow? Tash's head was down, and though she wasn't exactly panting, she was breathing hard. Pushing Pa was a real workout.

Pa himself seemed oddly cheerful. Clancy wasn't sure he even realised that the police were chasing them, or that Agent Melissa had evicted him from his own house. They passed the hairdresser, the pizza place, the bakery, the café. Clancy wondered if Tash would stop to buy Pa a coffee; they hadn't had breakfast. But Clancy's stomach was clenched tight with worry, and the thought of food made her queasy.

Eventually Tash parked the wheelchair behind the shelter of a tree.

'Tash, if we can't call a taxi, how are we going to take Pa back to The Elms?'

'No, no!' Pa looked dismayed. He waved his hand back toward the hills, in the direction of his house.

'We can't stay here, Pa,' said Tash.

'Sp-sp-sp?'

'We just can't,' said Tash crossly.

'So, back to The Elms,' said Clancy.

'Use your peabrain,' said Tash. 'By the time we get there, the police will have tracked us down and they'll be waiting for us. With *warrants*. We'll be arrested.' She lowered her voice. 'Like Mark.'

Clancy shot an anxious glance at their grandfather, who wasn't supposed to know about Mark, but it was all right. Pa wasn't listening; he was watching a flight of rainbow lorikeets swoop overhead. Under cover of their raucous screams, Clancy whispered, 'But you said we weren't doing anything wrong! You said it was all legal!'

Tash shrugged. 'What do I know? That woman seemed pretty upset.' She leaned across to hiss in Clancy's ear, 'And Mum's not here to bail us out. Or even Polly. And now they'll probably get into trouble for leaving us on our own, too.'

Clancy screwed up her face. 'Could we take Pa back, and then just run away?' she whispered. 'They wouldn't arrest *Pa*.'

'But will The Elms even take him back? Remember what that nurse said?'

'Neneh.'

'Whatever. If they already think he's too much trouble, what are they going to say when the police turn up?'

'But they can't just kick him out! Can they?'

Tash spun their grandfather around to face them. 'You don't want to go back to The Elms, do you, Pa?'

Mum would call that leading the witness, thought Clancy, and sure enough, Pa agreed, 'No, no, no.'

He hunched over in his chair, and Clancy looked at Tash, horrified.

'Pa's crying!'

'I have eyes,' snapped Tash. She knelt beside Pa's chair and gently took his hand. 'We won't take you back there, I promise. You can come and live with us.'

'With *us*?'

'Why not?' Tash straightened up and nodded across the highway. 'The railway station's over there. We can catch a train to the city, then tram it back to our place.'

'Sp-sp-sp!' Pa clutched at Tash's hand, his eyes shining.

'See?' said Tash. 'Pa thinks it's a good idea.'

'I didn't say it was a bad idea,' said Clancy hastily, though she couldn't imagine Pa and his wheelchair bumping around inside their tiny apartment. In four years, he had never even come for a visit. But at least there was a lift in their building, so there would be no problem with stairs. And Pa would be safe there until Tim and Harriet and Bruno arrived back from New Zealand. They might even be back tomorrow, she thought hopefully. Just one more night...Then Tim and Harriet could sort everything out.

As long as the police didn't catch up with them first. Or Agent Melissa. Or Polly. Sooner or later, Melissa was going to talk to Polly...

So now it was official. They were on the run.

13

Tash used some of Pa's biscuit tin money to buy them all train cards and load them up with cash.

'It's like buried treasure,' said Clancy. 'From Pa's pirate past. Pa's perfidious pirate past.'

'Yeah, Pa was a pirate.' Tash rolled her eyes.

'He only has one leg – well, one leg that works properly.' Clancy was tempted to add something humorous about parrots, but she could see that Tash still wasn't ready for humour. 'Tash, I'm really, really sorry about your phone.'

'One more thing you've ruined, ruiner. You can buy me a new one.'

Clancy eyed her sister sideways, unsure if this was supposed to be a joke or not. If she could have had that one wish now, she would have used it in a heartbeat to fix Tash's phone. She closed her eyes and imagined all the shattered pieces leaping back into place, like in a video run backward. But that really would be magic. Not even Nan's ghost could manage that.

Meanwhile, no phone meant no phone calls, no texts, and no way to tell Tim or Harriet or Polly where they were, even if they weren't sure they wanted them to know. A chill trickled down Clancy's spine. Technically Pa was an adult, so they weren't actually all alone. But really, Pa needed more taking care of than they did, so did he still count as an adult? At least Tash was here to tell Clancy what to do. Tash was capable, Tash was responsible, Tash was brave. Their parents said that often enough. So all Clancy had to do was follow her sister's orders, right?

The train came thundering into the station. Tash gripped the handles of the wheelchair as the train roared by, slowing as it slid along the platform. Pa clutched the arm of his chair tightly as Tash trundled him toward the nearest set of doors. Clancy hurried to open them.

'Careful, Tash, there's a massive gap.'

'I've got it,' said Tash grimly, tilting the chair back.

'Whoa!' cried Pa.

'Tash, watch out!'

'*Help* me then!'

'I can't – I don't—'

Before Clancy had a chance to do anything, a brown-skinned young woman in a hijab darted out of the train and grabbed the frame of the wheelchair to help Tash lift it up and over the gap and safely into the carriage. A whistle blew, Pa cried out urgently, Tash leapt on board and Clancy scrambled after her just in time as the doors hissed shut.

The train jolted and Clancy was thrown against the rail near the doorway. The wheelchair rolled and Pa gave another cry of alarm.

'I've got you, I've got you.' The young woman in the hijab guided the chair into a secure corner and expertly flipped on the brakes.

'I can do that!' said Tash.

'It's no problem.' The woman sat down and smiled at Pa. 'You're supposed to ask the station staff to bring out a ramp, you know. You're supposed to get on at the front, near the driver.'

'We didn't know,' said Tash defensively. 'We've never been on a train before.'

'Never been on a train?' The woman raised her eyebrows at Pa, who shrugged his shoulder, shook his head, and indicated his wheelchair.

'Not since his stroke,' said Tash. 'He's been on trains before. And so have we. Obviously. But not with him.'

The woman smiled at Pa. 'She doesn't give you a chance to say very much, does she?'

'Our grandfather can't talk.' Clancy jumped in to defend her sister as she would never have defended herself. 'He can understand everything you say, but he's got – um—'

'Aphasia,' growled Tash.

'Oh, okay. That's so sad.'

The woman smiled at Pa again, but this time it was not a playful, conspiratorial grin, but a pitying smile, and suddenly Clancy felt furious. Yes, it sucked that Pa couldn't walk, or speak when he wanted to, or even push his own wheelchair with his one good hand (not far, anyway), or live in his own house anymore. But this woman didn't even know him. How dare she feel sorry for him. How dare she look at him like that!

'He's fine!' said Clancy loudly. She laid her hand on Pa's bony shoulder, and he reached up to give it a pat.

'Sp-sp-sp,' he said soothingly, and the young woman suddenly became very busy looking at her phone.

At the next station, more people climbed on board. Even though it was summer holidays, the train was almost full of commuters. Tash and Clancy were crowded up against the wheelchair, shielding Pa. Some people glared at them, as if his chair were taking up precious space that actually belonged to regular travellers. Tash glared right back at them.

Clancy wished she was brave enough to do the same. Instead, she stared rigidly into the middle distance and avoided catching anyone's eye while being jostled helplessly this way and that by taller, heavier bodies.

Are we doing the right thing, Nan? she asked silently, but realised even as she formed the thought that she couldn't see out of the windows; she wouldn't be able to see a sign from Nan even if her grandmother sent one.

But then, just for a second, she caught a whiff of lily-of-the-valley. She twisted her head hopefully, but the scent had vanished. If she told Tash, her sister would probably say that it was coming from one of the other passengers. But Clancy felt comforted.

The journey from Rosella to the city took an hour. When the train pulled into the central station at Flinders Street, at last, the squashed-in passengers burst from the doors as if a cork had popped, and scattered in all directions. Clancy was swept out onto the platform by the flood of people.

'Tash? Tash!'

She turned and tried to fight through the crowd, but she couldn't push her way back onto the train. She was too small, and she couldn't see. What if this wasn't where Tash had wanted to get off? How would she ever find them again?

But then, even in her panic, she caught sight of Tash, carefully backing Pa out of a different doorway with the help of a big burly red-haired man in a hi-vis vest. 'No worries, love,' said the man cheerfully as he strode away.

Tash was scanning the crowd, peering back inside the train, swivelling her head in all directions. 'Clancy?' she called.

The doors sighed shut. The train was moving.

Tash screamed, '*Clancy*!'

'I'm here, I'm here!'

Pa touched Tash's elbow and pointed as Clancy hurried over, waving.

Tash grabbed her arm and shook her. 'Where were you? I couldn't see you! We have to stick *together*. Why didn't you get off with us?'

Tash freaking out was more scary than nearly being lost. Clancy's throat tightened, and tears blurred in her eyes. Pa patted her arm, then Tash's, and pantomimed wiping his brow. 'Phew!'

The train had roared away now, and the press of people was thinning out. Clancy wiped her face on her sleeve as Tash stared up and down the platform.

'Okay. No police.'

'Yay,' said Clancy weakly. 'We made it.'

'So far,' said Tash sternly. 'We *have* to stick together.'

'Like glue. Like magnets. Like gravity, holding planets in orbit—'

'It's not funny, Clancy!'

'I wasn't trying to be funny.'

'I mean it. If we get separated, with no phone—' Tash didn't finish the sentence. Pressing her lips together in a firm line, she grasped the wheelchair handles, and pushed.

14

Tash took Pa into the disabled toilet at the station while Clancy waited outside. Sometime, she guessed, maybe sometime soon, it would be her turn to hold the wheelchair while Pa hauled himself up and onto the loo, her turn to pull the chair out of the way and turn her back while he did what he had to do, to manoeuvre the chair back into position when he was done, and wheel him to the basin to wash his hands – or hand, in Pa's case. But until Tash insisted, Clancy wasn't going to volunteer. This was one eldest-grandchild privilege that Tash was welcome to hang onto as long as she wanted it.

Clancy glanced up at the clock on the concourse. It was just before nine. If this had been a normal summer holiday morning, she wouldn't have even been awake yet.

The sun slanted between the buildings and the glass of the skyscrapers dazzled white and gold. Seagulls wheeled above the slow brown ribbon of the river, pigeons strutted on the pavement, and sparrows darted for crumbs. Plenty of birds for Pa to look at, anyway.

Was the moon still there? Was Nan still watching over them, now that they'd left Rosella? There had been that hint of lily-of-the-valley on the train, but another sign would be reassuring. Clancy tried to catch a glimpse of the full moon between the towers as she followed Tash and Pa along the main street, but she couldn't see it anywhere. She was so intent on peering up at the distant wedges of sky that she walked into Tash's back.

'What are you *doing*?' said Tash crossly.

Clancy thought quickly. 'Just – looking for somewhere to eat. I'm starving.'

They were passing a fast food outlet. Tash said scornfully, 'We can do better than that.'

'Sp-sp-sp,' said Pa to himself. *Well, I wouldn't mind.* Clancy guessed he didn't get Maccas at The Elms.

Pa gazed happily round at the shops and signs and pedestrians hurrying past. A fruit stall glowed with apples and oranges; buckets of flowers sparkled with dew. The smell of frying bacon and hot chips followed them down the street, and Clancy's mouth watered.

Clancy soon gave up looking for the moon. She was so nervous about losing Pa and Tash in the big, noisy, confusing jumble of people and traffic and streets and buildings that she kept close to her sister, almost treading on Tash's heels as she pushed Pa's wheelchair steadily up the street, past the cathedral and the town hall, past souvenir shops and shoe shops and banks and clothing stores, weaving the wheelchair between tourists and students and skateboarders, buskers and beggars and businesspeople in suits.

'Down here.' At the top of the hill, Tash steered the wheelchair down a skinny side street, round a corner, and then another, into an even narrower laneway.

'This is it.' Tash tipped Pa's wheelchair up a low step and into a tiny Japanese café that Clancy would never have noticed. The miniature lettering on the front window read *Breakfast in Kyoto*.

The whole café was not much bigger than their cluttered living room at home, crowded with little wooden tables and cherry-red stools. Strings of silken red blossoms were looped across the walls, and paper lanterns dangled from the ceiling. Pa's wheelchair nudged the flimsy furniture aside like a whale nosing through a school of dolphins. A few solitary customers sat by the walls, hunched over laptops and teapots. A pale freckled girl stood guard over the register; she wore a black T-shirt, and tattoos swirled over her arms and up the side of her neck.

Tash gave her a brilliant smile as she steered Pa to a corner table. 'Hi! Is Josie working today?'

The pale girl shook her head. 'Tomorrow.'

'Oh, too bad. She's a friend of mine.' Tash flashed the brilliant smile again. This was a side of her sister that Clancy didn't often get to see in action – public Tash, social Tash, charming Tash.

But her charm seemed wasted on the pale-skinned girl. 'Oh, yeah? That's nice.' She laid two menus down on the table.

Tash handed them straight back to her. 'We'll have the breakfast special for three, thanks.'

When the waitress had gone, Tash reverted to the sister Clancy knew. She thrust the backpack into Clancy's arms and hissed, 'I'm going to the toilet. Can you manage to not throw this under a truck while I'm gone?'

Hurt, Clancy pulled up a stool, hugging the bag to her chest.

'Sp-sp-sp?'

'I don't know,' Clancy whispered back. What did people eat for breakfast in Japan, anyway? Clancy wasn't a massive fan of Japanese, or Thai, or even Chinese food. Just because her mother was Chinese, why did people always assume she'd love Asian food? Whatever this waitress was about to bring them, Clancy was sure it wouldn't be anything she'd want to eat. Almost definitely not cereal.

The girl who wasn't Josie reappeared with a jug of water and three glasses. Clancy noticed she had dark eyeliner tattooed beneath her eyes to give them an upswept look. That must have really hurt.

'Sp-sp-sp?' Pa held out his left hand for the waitress to shake. He loved meeting new people.

Pa looked expectantly at Clancy. Embarrassed, she mumbled, 'This is Godfrey. My grandfather.'

'Cool name. Nice to meet you.' The waitress shook his hand, and her eyes slid from Clancy to Pa and back again.

No, he's not Asian, Clancy felt like yelling at her. *Our mum is Chinese-Australian. Want to see my birth certificate?*

But the waitress didn't ask. She drifted away as a customer got up to pay, and Clancy stared at the table, her cheeks hot. She was sure that everyone in the café was staring at her and Pa.

At last Tash came back, damp around the edges of her face and hair as if she'd just had a good wash.

'So what *is* the breakfast special?' asked Clancy.

'It's Japanese,' said Tash briskly. 'You'll love it.'

'No, I won't,' muttered Clancy.

'Soz.' Tash shrugged. 'You could have ordered something else.'

Yeah, right, thought Clancy.

When the food arrived, Clancy was duly unimpressed. There was a large bowl of white rice, small bowls of brown broth, a pot of green tea, and a plate of little yellow parcels that turned out to be rolls of omelette.

Clancy sniffed at the broth. 'What's this?'

'Miso soup.'

'Sp-sp-sp?' said Pa.

'It's super healthy. Full of antioxidants.'

'What are the green bits?'

'Seaweed.'

'For *breakfast*?'

'Pfft!' But Pa was game to try anything, and when Tash dipped an omelette in the soup, he eagerly copied her. 'Mm!'

Resigned, Clancy filled a bowl with plain rice and sprinkled it with soy sauce. 'The first thing I'm going to do when we get home is make myself a *giant* bowl of cereal.'

Tash poured herself a tiny cup of green tea. 'Yeah, about that...'

Clancy's stomach, which had been feeling almost normal again with some food inside it, plunged like a rollercoaster. She put down her fork. 'What?'

'I don't think we can go back to our place.'

'What?' said Pa.

'Think about it. How could we carry the wheelchair up onto the tram? And then how would we lift it down again at our stop? Even the train was a nightmare, and that was all on one level.'

'We could walk there,' said Clancy desperately.

'You think? Okay, you can push.'

'Call another taxi then. We can borrow someone's phone—'

'I thought of that. That's why I was hoping Josie would be here. But she isn't. Anyway—' Tash leaned across the table and lowered her voice. 'It's not safe. The police must have our descriptions out by now, and they'll have found out our address. Big data, you know. They're probably staking out our place *right now*.'

'Sp-sp-sp?' Pa looked bewildered.

Tash stabbed an omelette roll with a chopstick. 'Also...' Clancy and Pa waited until she'd swallowed. 'I've been thinking, and I don't reckon Pa could live at our place. Our flat isn't even big enough for us. Where would he sleep? On the couch?'

Pa bowed his head. 'I – understand,' he whispered, one of those rare times when the words emerged all by themselves.

'So...' said Clancy. 'What are we going to do now?'

Tash scowled. 'I don't know. Why do I have to be the one who thinks of everything?'

Clancy stared at her. 'Because you're good at it!'

'Well, I'm sick of it. Someone else's turn.'

Clancy blinked at her bowl. Tash knew perfectly well that Clancy never had ideas, and even if she did, she wasn't brave enough to carry them out. Clancy was not born to be an outlaw. Being fugitives on the run seemed exciting on television. But in real life, it wasn't much fun at all.

'If you dare cry,' said Tash through gritted teeth, 'I will personally wring your neck.'

Clancy sniffed, and heroically managed to hold in her tears. Pa groped in the back pocket of his wheelchair and handed her a tissue.

'I'll pay.' Tash opened the backpack and pulled out the biscuit tin. It was hard to be discreet in the tiny café, and Clancy was aware of the pale waitress staring. Tash glared back at her as she tucked the tin away and took some notes across to the register.

'Wow,' said the waitress, holding the money. 'That's a lot of cash you've got in there.'

Other customers were watching now, over the tops of their screens, or twisted round on their stools.

'Yeah,' said Tash. 'It belongs to our grandfather. He doesn't like cards, he likes cash. You got a problem with that?'

'It just seems like a *lot* of cash, you know?'

'What, you think we stole it or something?'

'I dunno. Did you?'

'No!'

Tash and the waitress stared at each other.

'Maybe,' said the waitress, after a pause, 'maybe it was stolen from a poor old man who can't look out for himself.' Slowly her hand moved toward the phone lying on the counter.

'Sp-sp-sp!' cried Pa indignantly. He grabbed the rim of his wheel and pulled. The wheelchair crashed into a table; Pa changed direction and knocked over a stool.

'Clancy!' yelled Tash.

Clancy seized the handles of the chair and clumsily shoved Pa toward the door. Tash pulled the door wide, they bumped up and over the step and then they were racing up the laneway, bouncing Pa over the cobbles. Tash nudged Clancy aside and took the handles herself.

'I didn't – even – get the change!' Tash panted as they ran.

'Sp! Sp! Sp!' said Pa jerkily over his shoulder.

Tash groaned. 'Yeah, you're right. I can never go back there again.'

15

Out in the strong summer sun, soaring towers of silver and glass glittered without mercy. The streets were glaring, dusty canyons, with no shade and nowhere to hide. Snatches of discordant music blared from shop doorways as they hurried past. And suddenly there seemed to be someone in uniform on every corner.

Tash called to Clancy over her shoulder, 'We need to get off the streets!'

Clancy glanced around wildly. The city was a mystery to her. She had no idea where to go.

Tash was already swerving the wheelchair down another side street, clearing the way with her cries of 'Excuse me! Wheelchair coming through!'

'Oh, Tash, no, not in there—'

Her sister was heading for the doorway to one of the big department stores.

'Nah, nah, nah,' protested Pa.

'Too noisy, too crowded!' wailed Clancy.

They halted in the middle of the narrow footpath

to argue about it. 'You got a better idea?' demanded Tash.

Clancy stared around desperately. *Nan, please, I need a sign!*

Then she saw it: a mural of a blazing comet, streaking high across a wall above an old office building. Her heart leapt, and she flung out her hand. 'This way!'

Without waiting to see if Tash followed her, she plunged through the crowd, across a side street and along the block until she reached the site of the mural. Where to now? Gazing around, she caught sight of the Blue Moon Jazz Club, and headed for that.

From the Lucky Star convenience store, to a Eureka flag with its five-star design outside a museum, to Planet Games, Clancy darted across the city, ducking down laneways, breasting waves of traffic, twisting this way and that to Nan's next cosmic clue. Tash followed at her heels, grunting with effort, almost knocking pedestrians off the pavements as she swerved the wheelchair after her sister.

At last the trail ran out. Clancy paused for breath, panting, frantically searching for another sign. But the moons and stars, planets and comets and asteroids, had all vanished.

Tash caught up. Her cheeks were red and her forehead gleamed with sweat. 'What are you *doing*? Where do you think you're going?'

'Nan – Nan's showing us the way—' stammered Clancy.

'*What*? Are you crazy?'

Tash sucked in a deep breath to give Clancy a proper blast, but before she could launch, Pa interrupted. 'Sp-sp-sp!' He twisted round in high excitement to tug at Tash's arm. 'Sp-sp-sp!' He pointed down a nearby laneway, and propelled himself toward it.

'What's down there, Pa?' said Tash.

'Sp-sp! Sp-sp!'

Puzzled, Tash pushed and Clancy followed as Pa directed them down the lane, around a corner, and through a maze of narrow alleys, until they found themselves standing at the threshold of a covered arcade.

'Aha!' cried Pa.

Tash stopped the wheelchair, and Clancy skidded to a breathless halt behind them.

The arcade was roofed with panels of cloudy glass, held aloft by a framework of slender steel. This corner of the city seemed to exist in a hidden pocket, hushed and deserted. The sounds of the surrounding streets faded to a distant murmur like the whisper of the sea.

'Sp! Sp!'

Slowly Tash pushed the wheelchair forward. The temperature inside the arcade seemed to drop about ten degrees, as if they'd entered a cavern, deep in the earth.

'Looks like a murderer's hideout,' whispered Tash with relish.

'It looks like—' Clancy stopped, and goosebumps prickled her arms. What it looked like was a magical alleyway, the kind of place where you turned around and discovered that a hundred years had passed in the blink of an eye. The kind of place where you could buy a wand or a dragon's egg. The kind of place where you might slip back in time. *Oh, please let it be a time-slip alley!* prayed Clancy. Surely Nan's clues had led them here for a reason. *Something* was going to happen.

Pa stared around intently. 'Ha!' He pointed triumphantly to a small, dark shopfront at the arcade's dead end.

Clancy read out the sign painted on the window in golden letters. '*The Magpie Bookshop. Rare, Antiquarian and Orphaned Books.*' She glanced doubtfully at Pa. 'It doesn't look open.'

Tash cupped her hands to peer through the darkened window. 'It looks like it hasn't been open for years.'

'Sp-sp-sp,' insisted Pa. He leaned forward and pushed at the door. It swung slightly ajar, and a faraway bell gave a silvery tinkle.

'I guess it is open,' muttered Tash, and she held the door wide while Clancy pushed Pa inside. Clancy's heart was beating fast. Whatever waited for them inside, she felt safer behind the shelter of Pa's wheelchair. She was glad Tash was there.

Inside, the shop was hushed and cool as a cave. Faint light filtered through the front window and gleamed softly on wooden shelves laden with multi-coloured books. There were no other customers, and Clancy wondered in a sudden panic if the shop really was open. What if the owner swooped at them out of the shadows, shrieking like an angry bat?

Just then, a tall, thin, elderly white woman did appear from the back of the shop and came sweeping toward them. She was dressed in what looked like black silk pyjamas, with a black beret perched on top of her fluffy silver-white hair. Cats-eye glasses rested on her long nose, and ropes of jet beads clinked and rattled softly as she advanced between the shelves with her hands outstretched.

'Do my eyes deceive me? Is that you, Godfrey? Godfrey Sanderson?'

Pa reached out his hand to her, making happy wordless noises. 'Ah! Hah! N-n-n!'

The old woman clasped his hand in both of hers, and Clancy saw her dark eyes, bright behind her glasses, quickly darting over the wheelchair, Pa's limp right hand, his uncombed hair, his tracksuit pants, his stretchy slipper-shoes.

Then she turned her piercing gaze on Clancy and Tash. 'And who are these delightful young people? Surely you must be Beatrice and Philippa?'

Pa shook with laughter at her mistake. 'Nah, nah, yeah, nah. Sp-sp! Sp-sp!' He beamed proudly.

'*Grandchildren*? So soon?'

'We're Tim's daughters,' said Tash.

'Thomasina and Clarice,' said Clancy shyly.

'Tash,' said Tash firmly, shaking the old woman's hand. 'And this is Clancy.'

'Sp-sp-sp,' Pa reminded them.

'And we've got a little brother, Bruno,' added Clancy. 'But he's in New Zealand.'

'Of course he is!' cried the old lady. She leaned forward to kiss Pa's whiskery cheek, the ropes of shining beads clicking and clacking against his chest. 'How time does race by...It's wonderful to see you, Godfrey. Why, it must be half a dozen years since you paid me a visit. And how is darling Stella? She's not with you today?'

Pa closed his eyes. 'Sp-sp-sp.' He pressed his hand to his heart. 'Sp-sp-sp.'

Clancy shot a horrified look at Tash, who cleared her throat.

'Nan died about five years ago,' she said awkwardly. 'And then Pa had a stroke.'

The old woman turned pale. Wordlessly she groped for Pa's hand and squeezed it. Pa pressed his hand to her cheek, and for a moment they were motionless, in a shared, frozen grief.

'I'm so sorry, Godfrey,' said the old lady at last, wiping her eyes. 'No wonder I haven't seen you for so long. Dear me.'

Tash said, 'So...you and Pa know each other?'

'*Obviously*,' muttered Clancy.

'Indeed, Godfrey and Stella and I have been friends for many, many years – since our schooldays! We travelled together, we had all sorts of adventures.' The old woman drew herself impressively to her full height. 'My name is Antonia Wildwood. Welcome to my domain.'

She flourished her hand grandly around The Magpie Bookshop. 'Good heavens,' she said. 'It's terribly gloomy in here.' She strode to the window and tugged up the half-drawn blind. Clancy blinked as light washed into the shop. Then Antonia flicked a switch by the door, and light bulbs flickered to life. Now the shop looked almost like any ordinary bookstore – except that everything was coated in a light layer of silvery dust.

Antonia Wildwood clasped her hands together. 'A reunion of old friends – and new friends, I trust?' She peered at Clancy and Tash over the top of her glasses. 'Do any urgent appointments claim your time, or would you be free to join me for a spontaneous repast?'

Clancy waited for Tash to reply, but Tash just gaped at Antonia blankly. Clancy realised with a shock that, for once, her sister felt out of her depth.

Timidly Clancy whispered, 'Do you mean – have lunch with you?'

Antonia beamed. 'That is precisely what I mean!'

'I guess we could hang out here for a while.' Tash shot a look at Clancy, and glanced meaningfully at the door. Message received: they'd be safer hidden in here than outside roaming the streets, where police officers were hunting for them.

Just at that moment, Clancy's stomach gurgled. Mortified, she flushed red. Pa burst out laughing.

'Splendid! I shall close the shop!' announced Antonia, though it was doubtful anyone would even notice. Tash visibly relaxed as Antonia strode across to the door, her silk pants swishing, to flip the lock. 'There! Now we shan't be disturbed!' She beamed around at her visitors, and just for a second Clancy wondered what they'd do if she turned out to be some kind of crazy serial killer...

She took a deep breath, and as she did, she smelled lily-of-the-valley, the strongest whiff of the scent yet. So Nan did want them to be here! Perhaps she was even here herself... Clancy glanced surreptitiously around, but the shop was too brightly lit now to be hiding any ghostly shadows.

Anyway, in an emergency, she and Tash together could probably take Antonia down. Tash was good at tackling, and Clancy could sit on her.

'Follow me!' Antonia led them to an almost hidden door at the back of the shop.

'You guys were all at school together?' murmured Tash to Pa, as Clancy clumsily steered the chair between the crowded bookshelves. 'Seriously?'

'Sp-sp-sp,' said Pa proudly. He pointed to Clancy, and held his hand parallel to the ground.

'You were my age when you all made friends?' guessed Clancy.

'Yes!' Pa thumped the arm of his chair. 'Sp-sp-sp!'

But Clancy struggled to imagine that. She wasn't stupid; she knew that Pa must have been young once, that he hadn't always been old and white-haired, paralysed and speechless. But she found it hard to picture Pa and Antonia and Nan being the same age as her classmates from school, hanging out together, making silly jokes and teasing each other, doing whatever kids did back in the olden days before the internet and social media and – wow, maybe even television! – had been invented.

They must have played football, Clancy decided. She knew *that* had been around for at least a hundred years.

16

At the back of the shop was a big, untidy, purple-painted room that seemed to be part storeroom and part living space. An enormous table sat in the middle of the room, overflowing with piles of old books. A fat tabby cat stared up at them balefully from a couch in one corner. In another corner was a kitchenette, with a sink and a microwave, a small fridge and a shelf of mugs.

Clancy halted in the doorway, unable to push Pa's wheelchair past the boxes and cushions and armchairs and books and baskets that blocked the way through the room.

'Oh, dear!' cried Antonia. 'Just push all that clutter aside, Thomasina, dear.'

Tash heaved up a box, staggering under its unexpected weight; but then she couldn't find a space to put it down. Meanwhile Antonia was sweeping books and mugs and newspapers off the table and onto the floor, or the chairs, or the couch, to clear a space at one end, while Clancy inched Pa into the room.

'There – our banqueting board is prepared!' Antonia eyed the tabletop. 'A little grimy, perhaps, but that's soon remedied.' She whisked a cloth over the table, and clouds of dust rose into the air. Pa broke into a coughing fit.

'I'm afraid I haven't had time for spring-cleaning lately,' said Antonia. 'And besides, I find myself in agreement with Quentin Crisp.'

'Who's that?' asked Tash.

'A very wise man. According to Mr Crisp, if one neglects one's housekeeping, after the first four years, the dirt doesn't grow any worse.' Antonia smiled benignly, but Clancy wasn't sure that she was joking. This room certainly looked as if it hadn't been tidied up for about fifty years, let alone four. Clancy picked up a newspaper from a chair so she could sit down, and saw that it was dated from several years ago. Fastidious Polly would have freaked out big time if she'd seen this place. But it was such a cheerful, colourful muddle of books and cushions and pictures and rugs that most of the time Clancy didn't really notice whether or not it was clean.

Antonia glided majestically to the kitchenette and began to open cupboards and peer into boxes. 'Now, let me see. What can I offer you by way of a celebratory repast?'

The cat stretched in a leisurely way, leapt off the table and wreathed hopefully around Antonia's ankles. Clancy bent down to stroke his fur, which the cat endured, staring at her with enigmatic amber eyes.

'Soup to begin, then risotto, and chocolate pudding for dessert,' murmured Antonia. 'Does that sound acceptable?'

'That sounds *stellar*,' said Tash.

'Sp-sp-sp?' said Pa.

'You shouldn't go to all that trouble just for us,' said Clancy awkwardly.

Antonia Wildwood waved her hand airily. 'It's no trouble at all, my dear Clarice! These days, I do all my cooking in mugs. It's miraculous! Each guest can choose what they please, portion control is automatic, and best of all, the washing-up is practically negligible.'

'That means almost non-existent,' whispered Clancy to Tash.

Tash scowled. 'I know!'

Antonia fanned packets of cup-of-soup mix on the table like a deck of cards. 'Tomato, chicken noodle, cream of mushroom, laksa, pea and ham…'

Tash wrinkled her nose, less enthusiastic now; she didn't approve of processed food. Clancy picked beef with noodles, Pa chose gourmet tomato with croutons, Tash eventually selected laksa, and Antonia had spring vegetable.

For their second course, Antonia managed to produce mugs of pumpkin risotto for Tash and Pa, and bacon and mushroom for herself. Clancy felt that she'd eaten enough rice for one day, so Antonia made her a cheesy muffin, also in a mug. Everything was cooked in the microwave.

'And now for pudding!'

The pudding was the best part. Clancy slipped off her chair to watch Antonia make it. She mixed together a heaped tablespoon of self-raising flour, a heaped tablespoon of sugar and the same amount of cocoa, then stirred in two tablespoons of milk.

'One minute in the microwave, and it's done!' Antonia whipped the mug from the oven with a flourish. 'Would you care to try your hand?'

'Oh, no.' Clancy stepped back. 'I can't cook. I'd mess it up.'

'Impossible! With the chef at your shoulder providing step-by-step directions? The secret is that you *must* stir the dry ingredients thoroughly – the elimination of lumps is essential.'

Clancy shook her head.

'I'll have a go.' Tash scraped out the last crumbs from the bottom of her mug. 'But, I have to warn you, I might need a few tries to get it perfect.'

After Antonia had made them all hot drinks – she had a tin containing every imaginable variety of tea – she dragged out a battered tin trunk and produced a shoebox filled with old photographs, all jumbled together, from tiny faded black-and-white squares to polaroids to glossy colour prints.

'Let me see – this was an experimental theatre group I belonged to for a time…Here I am with Juan in Buenos Aires…That was my old motorcycle. I rode it all the way across Communist Russia…'

'Wow,' said Tash. 'You really got around.'

'Ah, this is what I was searching for.' Antonia plucked out a slightly blurred photograph of three young people standing in a park with their arms around each other. 'Do you recognise yourself, Godfrey?'

'With a *beard*?' shouted Tash. 'No *way*!'

Clancy leaned across the table to look. The photo showed a young man with a sandy-coloured beard standing between two young women. One, tall and thin, with wild dark hair, huge sunglasses and a flowing red dress, was still recognisable as Antonia. The other woman was shorter, plumper than Antonia, with a round, dimpled face and soft, curling brown hair.

Clancy knew the answer before she asked, but just to make sure, she tapped Antonia's arm. 'Who's this?'

'Sp-sp-sp!' cried Pa. He pointed to Clancy, to Tash, to himself.

'That's Nan, of course,' said Tash. 'Peabrain. Who else would it be?'

'Darling Stella.' Antonia smiled sadly.

Clancy picked up the photograph, and summoned her courage. 'Would it be okay if – could I keep this?'

Antonia turned to Clancy, surprised, and gave her a piercing look over the top of her spectacles. 'Of course. Unless you want to to take it, Godfrey?'

Pa gently tapped his temple. 'Sp-sp-sp.'

Antonia smiled. 'Take it, Clarice. Your grandfather and I don't need photographs. We have our memories.'

When Antonia left the room to go to the toilet, Clancy whispered to Tash, 'I think we should ask Antonia what to do. You know, about Pa, and – everything.'

Tash scowled. 'Why? We're doing all right on our own.'

'Oh, yeah? So what are we going to do next?'

Tash's scowl deepened. 'I haven't decided yet.'

'We could at least *ask*—' Clancy broke off as Antonia returned. She stopped and smiled when she saw that Pa had drifted off to sleep in his chair, with Louis the cat curled on his lap.

'Poor Godfrey!'

'He didn't sleep very well last night,' explained Clancy.

'Oh dear, why was that?'

Tash glared at her sister. 'No particular reason.'

Clancy gave Tash a pleading look. But Tash just folded her arms. Obviously she wasn't going to cooperate. It was up to Clancy. She summoned up the memory of that shooting star at Rosella, the signs and signals that had brought them here, and the clear scent of lily-of-the-valley in the bookshop. She took a deep breath.

'Antonia – I think we should tell you what's really going on.'

17

'Oh, my.' Antonia set down her mug of peppermint tea, looking faintly alarmed. 'What a sinister beginning. You're not in trouble with the law, I trust?'

'Well – we kind of are.' Clancy shot a look at Tash. 'We've kidnapped Pa and the police are after us and we don't know what to do.'

'Dear me!' Antonia rose abruptly and glided out into the shop, her beads clinking. A moment later she was back. 'I have bolted the door, just in case. Now I think you'd better tell me the whole story.'

It all tumbled out. Tim and Harriet and Bruno rushing off to New Zealand to rescue Mark. Polly running away to Sydney. The mass escape from The Elms. And at last, the three of them fleeing from Rosella with Agent Melissa and the police on their trail.

The only part of the story that Clancy kept to herself was Nan's helping hand. She wasn't sure yet if Antonia was the kind of person who believed in ghosts and magic;

but she knew that Tash wasn't, and she couldn't face her sister's mockery again.

'My heavens.' Antonia wrapped her hands around her mug with a troubled expression. 'It does sound like a delicate situation.'

Tash leaned across the table and spoke for the first time. 'The main thing, the crucial thing, is that Pa can't go back to The Elms. When we talked about taking him back there, he cried. So we have to find him somewhere else to live.'

'The obvious solution would be that he moved in with Timothy and the rest of your family…No?'

'Our apartment is way too small,' said Clancy. 'I'm even sharing a room with Bruno.'

'I see…'

Then Clancy had a blinding idea. *This* was why Nan had led them to Antonia! 'He could live with you!' she cried. 'How cool would that be?'

'Sh!' Tash glowered at her and Clancy guiltily clapped a hand over her mouth as Pa stirred in his sleep; but he didn't wake.

Clancy gazed hopefully at Antonia, but she was shaking her head. 'I wish I could help, my dear, sincerely I do. But I'm afraid these premises are hardly suitable. Strictly speaking, I'm breaking council regulations by living here myself. I don't even have proper bathroom facilities. It's a lick and a promise for me most days, I'm sorry to say. No, I don't think Godfrey would be at all comfortable here.'

Clancy sank back in disappointment.

'We're open to ideas,' said Tash. 'We're getting kind of desperate, to be honest with you.'

'Let me consider.' Antonia folded her hands, closed her eyes, and sat quite still. Louis' rhythmic purrs and Pa's gentle snoring filled the silence.

'Whenever you're ready,' said Tash.

Antonia raised an imperious hand. 'Quiet, please! I'm cogitating.'

Thinking, mouthed Clancy.

I know! Tash mouthed back. They glared at each other.

The room was very still. Outside the bolted door, beyond the shelter of the arcade, the city seethed and baked in the afternoon heat. But the cave of The Magpie Bookshop was hushed and still.

Clancy had once done a school project about an ancient priestess called an *oracle*, who lived in a cave. People had travelled from the ends of the world to hear her prophecies. Even if Antonia couldn't be their saviour, perhaps she could be their oracle. As long as she hadn't fallen asleep too...

Clancy was just leaning forward to check, when Antonia's eyes flew open.

'Godfrey and Stella have five children, correct?'

Tash nodded. 'Polly's the oldest, I think, then Dad, then Mark, then the twins.'

'Are any of the others in a position to assist? What about Pauline?'

'Polly's house has too many steps,' said Clancy. 'And she and Pa would drive each other crazy. Polly's neat. Pa gets bored when things are too organised.' Tash was staring at her. 'What? It's true.'

'Yeah, maybe,' murmured Tash doubtfully.

'And Mark?' asked Antonia. 'Has he relocated permanently to New Zealand?'

'Unless he gets deported,' said Tash. 'But he's probably in jail. So he's useless.'

'We never see Dad's family,' said Clancy. 'We hardly even know them. I'd never been to Polly's house till the other day.'

'They all used to come home for Christmas – to Rosella, I mean,' said Tash. 'But that hasn't happened since Nan died. Obviously. They're all over the place.'

Antonia nodded. 'Yes, Stella always was the glue that held the family together.' She tilted her head. 'The twins were born somewhat later than the rest, were they not? But if you two are so grown up, they must be almost adults by now?'

'Oh, totally adult,' said Tash.

'They're like, really old,' Clancy assured her. There was no distinction in her mind between her parents' age (forty-something) and her twin aunts' (thirty-something).

'Old enough to share in some responsibility for caring for Godfrey? Although I expect they are busy with their own lives.'

Tash looked at Clancy with sudden hope. 'I never thought of Bee and Pip.'

'Do we know where they live?' said Clancy, doubtful.

'Godfrey would know, surely?'

'He can't spell anymore,' said Tash. 'So even if he does know, he can't tell us and he can't write it down.'

'Could he point on a map, maybe?' said Clancy.

'There may be a simpler way to find out.' Antonia scraped her chair back and vanished into the shop. A few moments later she returned with a fat book printed on very thin paper.

'The telephone directory,' she said, seeing the girls' blank looks. 'I suppose these are almost obsolete by now. As will be books in general soon, I fear.' She sighed. 'Let me see, we'll begin with Beatrice, shall we? Sanderson, Sanderson...Oh, dear, there are quite a few...'

'I could have done this a lot quicker if I still had my phone.' Tash scowled at Clancy.

'It was an *accident*.' Clancy got up to peer over Antonia's shoulder. 'Well, we know it's not Mr B Sanderson – that cuts out a few of them.'

Tash leaned over Antonia's elbow. Suddenly her finger shot out to jab the page. 'That's her! I'm sure that's her, in Docklands. Didn't she buy a flat there? Remember

Dad saying we could watch the New Year's Eve fireworks from there? Not that we ever did.'

'But – that's not far from here, is it?' said Clancy.

Tash straightened up, her eyes bright. 'Yep. We're nearly there.'

18

The next step, clearly, was to call the number, which Tash did, on Antonia's telephone at the counter in the shop. But Tash only listened for a moment, then hung up.

'What? Was it not Bee?'

'Disconnected. But that doesn't mean anything,' said Tash determinedly. 'Who has a land line anymore?'

Clancy thought of something else. 'She'd be at work now, anyway.'

'Good point. I think we'll have to go round there and wait.'

Clancy's stomach clenched. She'd just started to feel safe in The Magpie Bookshop and now Tash was going to rip that away. 'Now?'

Tash considered. 'Maybe Friday night isn't the best time to drop in,' she conceded. 'She might be going out. Or she might be too tired after working all week. Tomorrow morning would be better.'

Now Clancy had something new to worry about. 'Have we got enough money for a hotel?'

But Antonia came gliding past in time to overhear her. 'You're welcome to spend the night with me, my dears, if you don't mind roughing it. I have plenty of bedding to spare.'

'That's really kind, thanks,' said Tash, at the same time as Clancy said anxiously, 'We don't want to be any trouble.'

Antonia waved away her worry. 'It gives me such pleasure to have you all here, Clarice. It reminds me of old times. We used to have a thriving community in the arcade, but one by one they all sold up and moved out. I'm the last one left, and I suppose I will be departing myself before long. They've offered me a considerable sum – developers, you know – but to be perfectly truthful, I can't face clearing out the shop. And I'm content to stay here a little longer . . . especially when friends still drop by.' She clasped her hands and smiled. 'Enough melancholy! Shall we go and see if your grandfather is awake?'

Pa was awake. He was bent over the table, deftly sorting through photographs with one hand. 'Sp-sp-sp!' Triumphantly he held up another picture of Nan to show Antonia.

'Ah, yes, that's Stella, and that is my friend Verity Wainwright, who owned the camera shop in the arcade. I believe Stella was one of her best customers. Do you know—' Antonia laid the photograph on the table as a thought occurred to her '—it was Stella who alerted me that this shop was for sale when I was first searching for suitable premises.'

'You mean, you only bought this shop because of Nan?' Clancy felt a click inside her brain, like a jigsaw piece slotting into place, or the moment when she guessed the plot twist before the end of a movie. Suddenly she became aware of a very faint aroma of lily-of-the-valley. If she turned around, would she see a shadowy figure in the corner of the room, watching them with love?

'What happened to Verity Wainwright?' asked Tash.

'Oh, she closed her shop and retired to Queensland... took the developer's money and ran, you might say.' Antonia sighed. 'Perhaps I should join her, who knows?'

'And if you sell up, what happens to the arcade?'

Antonia waved her hand. 'It will vanish in a cloud of dust, and like a phoenix from the ashes, a new building will take its place. That's the way of the world, the old makes way for the new. It's inevitable.'

Entropy again, thought Clancy; old buildings falling into ruins or being knocked down. It took much more energy from the universe to put together a complicated structure like a house, or a book, or a wheelchair, than it took to destroy them or let them fall apart.

It made Clancy sad to think of the lovely old arcade being bulldozed and some boring office block replacing it. Wiped out, as if it had never existed. Would the ghost of the arcade haunt the new building? The city must be full of phantom buildings...big Victorian hotels and theatres, old shops, back and back to the very first houses of the white settlers, and before them, the shelters of the Wurundjeri people who had camped and fished beside the river for thousands of years... Clancy shivered. She hoped all the ghosts were friendly ones, like Nan.

It must be making Nan's spirit happy to see Pa and Antonia laughing together, sharing memories. Even Clancy could remember how happy Nan had been at Christmases, when everyone was together, joking and reminiscing and eating roast potatoes and turkey. Nan must have been so sad that all her children had drifted apart, like stars drifting away from each other, out into the cold vastness of the universe.

Could the same thing happen to her and Bruno and Tash one day? It was a shocking thought. Annoying as they might be, she couldn't imagine not seeing her sister and brother every day; it had been weird enough without Bruno for the last few days. She definitely couldn't imagine not even knowing where her siblings lived, the way Dad hadn't known that Mark was in New Zealand. Cold fingers seemed to close around her heart.

Antonia said they could make beds on the floor of the shop out of sofa cushions. 'But you must solemnly vow not to betray my secret to the council. I wouldn't care to be evicted at this late stage.'

'Of course not!' said Tash indignantly.

'We're outlaws, too,' Clancy reminded her.

Pa zipped his hand solemnly across his lips, which made them all smile, because he couldn't have told anyone even if he wanted to, though Clancy thought it might have been interesting to watch him try.

'What about Pa?' she asked suddenly. 'He can't sleep in the chair again, and he can't sleep on the floor. With his wobbly leg, he'd never get up again.'

'My sofa folds out into a perfectly adequate double bed,' said Antonia. 'If Godfrey doesn't object to sharing with an old friend.'

'Pfft!' Pa waved away any objections.

'We'll go and visit Bee tomorrow,' Tash told him. 'In her flat at the Docklands. I bet she has an amazing view. Are you excited?'

Pa nodded emphatically, and pressed his hand to his heart.

But later, when Tash and Clancy were making up beds between the bookshelves in the shop, where Pa couldn't hear, Clancy whispered, 'Why did you tell him we were just going for a visit? I thought we were checking out if Pa could move in with Bee forever?'

'We are. We will. But I don't want Pa to be too disappointed if she says no. *But*,' said Tash, 'it'll be that much harder for her to say no to his face.'

'Okay,' said Clancy doubtfully. As usual, Tash seemed very confident. And perhaps this was the answer Nan had been leading them toward all along. She guessed there was only one way to find out.

19

That night Antonia made them noodles in mugs for dinner, and another microwave cake, this time with strawberries and cream, for Tash and Pa. Clancy had chocolate pudding again, which Tash made for her, but despite Antonia's encouragement and Tash's jeers, Clancy still didn't dare to try making it herself.

Antonia said, 'You are welcome to use my telephone, Thomasina. I would hate to think of your parents being anxious about you.'

'Well, I'd *like* to ring them,' lied Tash. 'But I don't know their numbers. You know what it's like – well, maybe you don't – all the numbers are just in your phone, you can't *remember* them.'

'I see. And you don't have them written down some-where?'

Clancy could tell that Tash was trying really hard not to roll her eyes. 'Yeah, I do. *On my phone.*'

Clancy jumped in to defend her sister. 'That's how it works. That's just life.'

Antonia and Pa exchanged a shrug, and Tash and Clancy looked at each other, united for once, one generation against another.

After dinner, Antonia and Tash helped Pa wash and get ready for bed, while Clancy unfolded the sofa and spread out the sheets. As the others settled Pa into bed, Clancy wandered to the back of the room and peered through the single window, set high in the wall. She could just glimpse a slender slice of the night sky, with the crescent moon suspended in it.

'Aww!' cried Tash, as Louis jumped onto the bed, curled himself on Pa's feet and began to purr. Pa gave everyone the thumbs-up, and Antonia ushered Clancy and Tash from the room. Pa's eyes were closed before they were even out of the door.

'Pa sleeps heaps more since he had his stroke,' Tash whispered in the doorway. 'His poor brain gets so tired.'

Antonia nodded. 'I understand. I daresay an early night will do us all good...But do feel free to explore the shop at your leisure, won't you. Help yourselves to anything you like. Good night, my dears, and sleep well.'

Tash wandered around the shop, pulling out the odd book and flicking through it, then placing it back on the shelf. She was not a great reader, and before long she threw herself down on the cushions and closed her eyes.

But Clancy saw so many tempting books, she couldn't decide which one to look at first. She found an entire shelf of astronomy books, including one by Neil deGrasse Tyson himself, and the companion book to the original *Cosmos* series back in the 1980s. The two books she finally selected to take to bed were a large square atlas of the southern sky, and a slim volume of Aboriginal stories about the constellations. But she wasn't reading for long before she found her own eyelids growing heavy.

With the lights off and the blinds drawn, Clancy lay next to Tash, surrounded by books in the dark. She could hear Antonia talking to Pa in the back room – at least, she could hear the murmur of Antonia's voice, and an occasional noise from Pa that might have been a drowsy chuckle or a snore. Once she thought she heard the same throaty laugh that she'd heard back at the house in Rosella...not Antonia's laugh, not Tash's laugh. The noise from the back room sounded like three old friends chatting quietly in the dark.

After a while, she heard the gentle rhythm of snoring, though whether it came from Pa, or Antonia, or both of them, she couldn't tell.

'Night,' mumbled Tash, and soon Clancy heard her sister's breathing slow and deepen, and knew that she was sleeping, too.

But Clancy lay awake, listening to the muffled noises of the city that seemed so far away, even though they were right in the midst of it all: sirens and traffic, and the whirr and clicking of pedestrian lights. Friendly shadows tiger-striped the inside of The Magpie Bookshop.

This was the weirdest place Clancy had ever spent the night, with shelves of old books rearing up the walls on every side. Muddled thoughts drifted through her mind, of the thousands of stories, poems, pictures, facts and words folded away inside the closed books...all those words, and still the number of words on all those pages wouldn't be as many as the number of stars in the universe...all those stars...and something about the moon...

Clancy knew that she was overlooking something important, but she was too foggy with tiredness to work out what it might be. In the end she decided that it must be bothering her that they hadn't been able to contact their parents all day, not even by text. Still vaguely troubled, she rolled over and closed her eyes.

A soft noise, a rustle of turning pages, made her shiver awake. She whispered into the darkness, 'Nan?'

Silence.

Which was, on balance, less scary than receiving an answer...

But a feeling of comfort and wellbeing wrapped around Clancy like an old dressing-gown, the darkness soft as feathers and faintly lily-scented. *I know you're there, Nan,* thought Clancy, and she was sure she could hear Nan's voice inside her head, whispering to her to *go back to sleep.*

She snuggled down and sank into a strange dream where the books stirred, their pages whispering, and her grandmother crossed the night-striped floor to open the door so that they could spread their covers and flutter out. Nan stood in the doorway, moonlight silvering her curly hair, watching as the books soared out like bats into the star-filled sky.

20

The moon.

It was the moon.

Clancy's eyes flew open. The bed of sofa cushions had split apart in the night and her hipbones were resting uncomfortably on the floorboards. She sat up. 'Tash!'

Her sister burrowed deeper into the bedding. 'Mmmph.'

'It's the moon, Tash. When we were at Rosella, it was full. But last night, it was only a crescent.'

'So?' mumbled Tash.

'So, the moon doesn't work like that. It can't jump from full to crescent in one night.'

'Well, you must be remembering it wrong then.' Tash sat up, pulled out her ponytail and crossly rubbed her hands through her hair. 'Maybe you dreamed it.'

But Clancy was sure she hadn't been dreaming, not last night, or the night before. 'Did you notice what the moon looked like?'

Tash looked at her. 'No, I did not notice what the moon looked like. I had more important things to think about.'

Clancy was vaguely sure that this *was* important, but she knew she wouldn't be able to convince her sister. She pushed the question of the moon's strange behaviour to the back of her mind; but she didn't forget.

An antique medical textbook was lying open on the floor at the foot of their makeshift bed; Clancy almost tripped over it. Not the bedtime reading she would have expected Tash to choose. Clancy slotted it back on the shelf.

It turned out that Antonia, drifting around in an embroidered silk kimono, which was only slightly grubby at the cuffs, was not really a morning person. She didn't have any cereal, or a toaster, and Clancy wasn't keen on any of the breakfast options that could be cooked in a mug. To be polite, she accepted the offer of coconut porridge, but she didn't like coconut, and she left most of it for Tash.

It took a long time to get Pa up. He was grumpy, and clumsy, and inclined to growl when Clancy tried to insert his strong arm into his shirt sleeve first, instead of the limp one, or when Tash approached the wheelchair to the bed at the wrong angle. By the time they had him dressed and sitting in his chair, everyone was feeling short-tempered, and even Tash could see that it might be best not to hang around too long.

After Clancy had folded up the rugs and quilts, and Tash had replaced the sofa cushions, Antonia gathered them in the back room to give out presents – books, of course.

For Pa, she had a guide to local birds. 'No doubt this is already part of your collection, but I thought you might enjoy leafing through it again.' Pa pressed it to his heart, blew Antonia a kiss, and tucked the book into the back pocket of his wheelchair.

For Tash, there was a volume of short stories by Margo Lanagan. 'Because I know you can't spare much time for reading. These are short, but I believe you'll find them an intriguing challenge.'

Last of all, Antonia turned to Clancy. 'Clarice, my dear, will you allow me to give you the star atlas?'

'Oh!' Clancy was overwhelmed. 'But – it must be worth a lot of money...'

Tash was blunt. 'We can't lug that massive book around with us. I mean, it's very generous, but—'

'How thoughtless of me! I quite understand. Perhaps Clarice would care to return to collect it another time?'

'That would be great,' said Clancy, relieved.

'But I can't have you going away empty-handed...' Antonia looked around for another idea.

Clancy found it very difficult to ask for things she wanted. She threw a desperate look at her sister, who grimaced, but came to her rescue.

'Antonia, I think Clancy found another book last night she'd like to keep, if that's okay.'

'It's only a little one,' said Clancy hastily, showing the slender book of legends to Antonia.

'By all means, keep it, my dear. But it seems such a meagre gift…' With a cry, Antonia pounced on the shoebox of photographs and extracted the top handful of pictures, the pictures of Nan when she was young, before she was anyone's mum or grandmother, when she was just Stella Sanderson.

'For me?'

Antonia nodded.

'But – don't you want to keep them? Or Pa?'

Pa gently pushed her hand away and shook his head. 'Sp-sp-sp.' *You take them.*

Antonia kissed their cheeks, and bent to give Pa a long hug. 'You will visit me again, won't you? If you can?'

'Sp-sp-sp,' promised Pa, and Clancy and Tash vowed that they would.

Tash pushed Pa's chair to the end of the arcade, where the line between the shadows and the bright sunlight was as sharp as a knife. They all turned to wave to Antonia where she stood outside The Magpie Bookshop in the empty arcade, a thin figure in black with her shining white hair.

'Wave, Pa!'

But when Clancy turned back for a final look, Antonia had disappeared, vanished like a ghost in the sunlight.

Clancy blinked. But the envelope of photographs was safe in her pocket, to prove that it had all really happened. As they wound their way through the tangle of alleys, she looked around hopefully for a sign from Nan: a star or a comet or even a spaceship.

But there was only the moon – the daytime moon, a pale wafer, crisp as a biscuit against the blue sky. And it was full.

Did that mean that the moon she'd seen last night was fake? A projection, or a neon sign? No. She knew the real moon when she saw it. But then how—?

'Clancy! Hurry up!'

Tash and Pa had already crossed the road, and Tash was beckoning impatiently.

Clancy dithered, then made her mind up. She yelled, 'Hang on a minute! Wait there!' And she turned and ran back down the street and through the labyrinth of narrow alleys back to the arcade.

But the arcade was gone.

Clancy ran to the corner of the glass and concrete office building with its funky yellow and orange tiles, scanned the street, and jogged back. She retreated, staring up at the blank-faced tower; but it told her nothing.

She ran back around the corner and through the maze of alleyways to the main road where Tash and Pa were waiting.

'Sp-sp-sp?' roared Pa crossly.

'I – I decided I wanted to take the star atlas with me after all,' stammered Clancy.

'Well, you'll have to carry it yourself then,' said Tash. 'So where is it?'

'I didn't get it.' Clancy took a deep breath. 'The book-shop's gone.'

'What do you mean, gone?'

'It's disappeared. The whole arcade's gone. There's an office building there instead.'

A flicker of something crossed Tash's face, too fast for Clancy to read. Was it disbelief? Or fear?

'You must have got lost,' said Tash. 'You're hopeless.'

'I didn't! If you don't believe me, go and look for yourself.'

'We don't have time. Anyway, you're being ridiculous. Of course the bookshop's still there.' Tash turned and started to march along the footpath, pushing Pa's chair in front of her.

'Tash!' wailed Clancy.

'Sp-sp-sp!' cried Pa. *Hurry up!*

Clancy gave up. She had to break into a trot to catch up with them.

The walk to Docklands was longer than they'd expected.

'Look at those hills!' groaned Clancy.

'How about you do some work for a change?' said Tash grimly, and the girls gripped one handle each to drive the wheelchair up the steep slopes, with Pa calling encouragement. 'Sp-sp!'

'What – number – is it?' panted Clancy, when they finally reached Bee's street.

'Eight hundred and something,' gasped Tash.

Clancy almost stopped dead. 'Five hundred to go?'

'Don't stop, don't stop!'

Block after block, hill after hill, they trudged on under the summer sun, sweat rolling down their backs, their legs aching, past towering skyscrapers, hotels and shops, and across railway tracks, as the numbers climbed higher. By the time they reached Bee's building, a glittering triangular shard of steel and glass, Clancy's knees were shaking so hard she thought she might fall over.

Luckily, someone was going out just as they were coming in, and held the door for them. (Later, Clancy decided that this was part of Nan's magic, too.) As they stepped inside the foyer, the air-conditioned atmosphere enveloped them like cool water.

'Sp-sp-sp!' Pa admired the shiny marble and glitzy tiles.

Clancy staggered toward some leather-covered benches. 'I need to sit down...'

'No! Come on, let's just get up there.' Tash seized the handles of Pa's chair and pushed him toward the lifts.

Clancy leaned weakly against the wall of the elevator as Tash punched the button for the tenth floor. 'I need a drink.'

'I need a shower.'

'I need some breakfast.'

'I need new sunglasses.'

'I need Band-Aids for my feet.'

'Sp-sp-sp,' scoffed Pa.

'It's all right for you. You're just sitting there!' said Tash, and Pa had to agree.

Clancy was still reeling from the disappearance of the arcade, and she was so hot and exhausted that she wasn't even feeling nervous about how they were going to explain themselves to Bee. That was Tash's job, anyway. Clancy trailed along the carpeted corridor after Tash and Pa, hoping vaguely that Bee had Band-Aids, and wondering what kinds of cool drinks she might keep in her fridge.

'Here we go.' Tash knocked at the glossy white door of Bee's apartment.

There was no response.

'Sp-sp-sp!' urged Pa, and Tash hammered at the door again.

Pa cocked his head. 'Sp-sp-sp?'

'I can hear her moving around,' agreed Tash, and she rapped on the door for the third time.

After what seemed like a very long moment, the door slowly swung open.

There was a pause while they all stared at one another.

It had been a few years since Clancy had last seen her youngest aunts. But even so, she knew at once that this wasn't Bee.

21

Pa was the first to break the silence. 'Sp-sp-sp?' he demanded. *Who the hell are you?*

Tash stepped in front of the wheelchair. 'We're looking for Beatrice Sanderson. Is she here?'

The person retreated, and narrowed the door until only a crack remained open. 'No. Sorry.'

'When's she coming back?' persisted Tash.

A suspicious eye peered out at them. 'She doesn't live here anymore.'

'*What?*' exploded Pa.

'But this is the right address? This is her apartment?'

'Was.' The voice became more distant, the crack narrowed, the face withdrew. 'She moved.'

'Wait a minute—' began Tash in agitation; then Pa tugged at her shirt and whispered, 'Sp-sp-sp...' He gestured to his lap.

'Oh, God. Sorry,' said Tash to the single visible eye. 'Can we use your toilet?'

There was a pause. 'I'm kind of in the middle of something.'

'It'll only take a second,' said Tash desperately. 'How can you turn away a disabled old man? Come on, please! You can see we're not axe murderers or anything.'

'But I'm busy,' said the voice feebly.

'Sp-sp-sp!' said Pa urgently.

And then Clancy, to her own horror, hot, tired, thirsty, hungry and confused beyond bearing, burst into tears.

The voice behind the door swore, in a resigned tone, and then pulled the door open wider. 'I guess you'd better come in then,' said the person gloomily, and Tash, Pa and Clancy trooped inside.

The inhabitant of Bee's apartment was a large person of indeterminate age and gender, wearing shorts and a T-shirt (Clancy guessed they'd probably slept in them), with dishevelled hair and glasses. 'The toilet's that way.'

Tash hurried Pa into the bathroom and left Clancy and the stranger staring awkwardly at each other, or rather staring awkwardly in different directions so they didn't have to talk. Clancy managed to gulp down her sobs and hastily wiped her eyes on the hem of her T-shirt. The flat was so small that they could hear every noise coming from the bathroom. Even if Bee had still lived here, thought Clancy, it was obvious that Pa could never have shared this tiny apartment with her. The place was a mess – empty pizza boxes, chip packets, dirty dishes, stinky clothes. Not like the pleasant muddle of The Magpie Bookshop, but squalor.

When the noises from the bathroom became embarrassing, the person cleared their throat. 'Looking for Beatrice?'

Clancy nodded, then, when more seemed to be required from her, she said, 'She's our aunt. Me and Tash's aunt. Not Pa's. She's his daughter. Our dad's sister. You know.'

'Right.' The person rocked on their heels.

Clancy sniffed desperately, and the person said abruptly, 'Hang on a sec.'

They marched off into what Clancy guessed was the bedroom, and emerged a few moments later with a rather squashed-looking box of tissues. 'Here you go.'

'Thanks,' said Clancy in a muffled voice, and blew her nose.

'You want a glass of water or something?'

'Yes, please.'

Eventually a clean (or clean-ish) glass was unearthed from the back of a cupboard, and Clancy gratefully gulped down tepid tap water. 'Thank you.'

The person squinted at her. 'You didn't know she moved to the country?'

'What? Bee? No.'

'Uh-huh.'

The toilet flushed, and after some bumps and scuffling, Tash emerged, pushing Pa's chair. Tash looked hot and cross, but Pa seemed pleased with himself, and gave Clancy a thumbs-up.

'Thanks for that,' said Tash. 'It was a bit of an emergency.'

'That's okay.' Abruptly the other person thrust out their hand. 'I'm Alex.'

'Hi, I'm Tash, and this is Clancy, and Godfrey.'

Clancy burst out, 'Alex says Bee moved to the country!'

'Seriously?' Tash pushed her hair back from her forehead. 'What did she do that for?'

Alex shrugged. 'Dunno. Tree change, I guess.'

'Sp-sp-sp?'

'Bee's moved to the country,' said Clancy. 'Did she move to a farm? Oh, Pa, how would you like to live on a little farm?'

'Sp-sp-sp,' agreed Pa.

'When did this happen?' demanded Tash.

'Few months ago.'

'Did you buy this flat from her?'

'Nah. Renting.' Alex had the grace to look embarrassed. They muttered unconvincingly, 'I was going to do a bit of a clean-up today.'

'That's okay, we won't tell her,' said Clancy.

'Sp-sp-sp?' Pa looked at his palm as if he were reading it. 'Ah!' He mimed scribbling something. 'Aha! Sp-sp-sp?' He looked at Alex expectantly.

Alex seemed faintly panicked. 'Um…'

'Sp-sp-sp! Sp-sp!'

Tash snapped her fingers. 'Bee's address! Have you got Bee's address?'

'Yes!' cried Pa. 'So-it-is!'

Alex ran their hand through their hair, making it stick up in frazzled spikes. 'Yeah, I've got it somewhere. It was on the fridge...'

They all turned at look at the fridge, which was completely covered in magnets, overdue bills, council notices, and takeaway menus.

'Or I can find it on my phone,' said Alex.

The phone was easier to find. It was eagle-eyed Pa who spotted it, half hidden under the couch. While Alex was checking back through their emails to retrieve Bee's address, Tash filled Clancy's glass with water for herself and Pa, and Clancy was able to duck into the bathroom, use the toilet, and give her face and hands a good wash.

Feeling much better, she came out into the tiny living room and looked out over the balcony for the first time. The view was breathtaking, across the sparkling water with its bobbing yachts, and back toward the spires of the city. She stammered something appreciative.

'What? Oh, you get used to it.' Alex shrugged. 'I hardly even notice it anymore.'

'It must look amazing at night,' said Clancy. 'Can you see lots of stars from here?'

Alex shook their head. 'Too much light pollution. It's pretty. But no stars.' They looked up from their phone. 'Got the address. Should I send it to you or what?'

'I don't have a phone,' said Tash. 'Anymore.'

'I'll write it down then.'

Which meant another hunt, this time for a pen and then for a scrap of paper. Clancy remembered her envelope of photographs (which was still in her pocket – which meant that Antonia and the bookshop weren't a dream...) and Alex carefully printed Bee's new address on the back.

'Quoll Creek,' they said. 'Gold rush country.'

Tash studied the envelope. 'What about a phone number?'

Alex shook their head. 'Haven't got one. Just the address.'

Pa looked around at the chaos of the flat and clucked his tongue. 'Sp-sp-sp,' he told Alex.

'Yeah, I know.' Alex slumped against the wall. 'But what can I do? It's out of control.'

'Sp-sp-sp.' Pa pointed to Tash and Clancy, and motioned them forward. *They'll help you!*

'Gee, thanks, Pa,' muttered Tash.

'Maybe we could help you throw stuff out,' murmured Clancy doubtfully.

Alex brightened. 'Would you? Really?'

'Sp-sp-sp!' said Pa.

Clancy looked at Tash. 'I think we owe Alex,' she said in a low voice. 'For letting us use the toilet. And drinks. And finding Bee's address.'

'Okay, okay.' Tash screwed up her face. 'What if we give you, I dunno, twenty minutes of full on throwing-out-crap time? But after that, you're on your own.'

'Deal,' said Alex.

They dug out a big black garbage bag and under Pa's supervision, the three of them rapidly filled it with rubbish. When in doubt, and when Alex was hesitating, Pa would give the final verdict with an emphatic, 'Yeah!' or 'Nah!', thumb up or thumb down, like a Roman emperor.

After twenty minutes, Clancy could see the carpet on the floor, and the couch had emerged from piles of discarded clothing, magazines, beer bottles and cereal bowls. Alex, Clancy saw with envy, had a great collection of cereal boxes (though a disappointing number of them were empty). The small round dining table was revealed, the sink was filled with dishes and Alex's laundry basket overflowed with washing.

'Sp-sp-sp.' Pa pointed to the sink. 'Sp-sp-sp.' He gestured to the laundry basket.

'Two jobs for today.' Alex heaved a giant sigh. 'I guess I could manage that.' They looked up hopefully. 'You don't want to give me a hand...?'

'We need to go,' said Tash firmly.

'Fair enough,' said Alex.

'Sp-sp-sp!' said Pa heartily, reaching out his hand to shake Alex's in congratulation.

'You'll be fine.' Clancy looked around the flat, impressed. Maybe no power in the universe could reverse the power of entropy, but it wasn't true that chaos was inevitable. Disorder could be transformed into order, more or less; all it took was a bit of energy. She let herself out onto the balcony to see if she could spot the arcade, or the building that seemed to have replaced it.

Alex joined her. 'I should thank you. I don't know what I would have done today if you three hadn't shown up.'

Clancy remembered. 'You said you were busy.'

'Mm.' Alex stared out at the city skyline. 'So I did.'

'Look!' Clancy's hand shot out. 'You might not be able to see any stars, but you can see the moon from here.'

'Huh,' said Alex. 'So you can. I should look out here more often.'

Clancy's heart filled with warmth as she gazed at the pale circle of the moon, hovering above the shining towers. Nan was still travelling with them. And what about Antonia?

Clancy wasn't sure if she'd just been lost and unable to find her way back to the arcade, or if The Magpie Bookshop was really gone. Then Antonia might have been inside her own little bubble of time, with her own phases of the moon, some time in the past before the arcade was knocked down. Clancy remembered that years-old newspaper in the back room. Perhaps it had been a time-slip alley after all... Now that really would be magic...

Well, whichever it is, thank you, Antonia. Thank you, Nan. She patted her pockets and the envelope of photos crinkled reassuringly under her hand.

'See you,' Alex called mournfully down the corridor as Tash trundled Pa back toward the lift.

'Bye!' Clancy called back.

'Sp-sp-sp?' asked Pa as the lift descended.

Tash said firmly, 'Food.'

22

It was practically lunch by the time they finally ate: fancy toast, pastries and coffee at a café busy with office workers. This time Tash managed to extract some money from Pa's stash of cash without attracting anyone's attention, but Clancy was still relieved when they made it out onto the street again without any awkward questions being asked.

'We can catch a train to Quoll Creek,' said Tash.

'Are you sure?' said Clancy.

'Of course! Easy!'

Tash and Clancy pushed Pa all the way back the way they'd come, up and down the same steep hills to Flinders Street station where they'd arrived the day before from Rosella – it felt like weeks ago now, not a single day.

Clancy waited with Pa in a sheltered corner outside the gates while Tash went to find out the platform for the Quoll Creek train. She was gone for a long time.

'Sp-sp-sp?' asked Pa.

'She'll be back in a minute,' said Clancy; but she eyed the big clock nervously as the minutes ticked past. What if there was only one train today, and they'd missed it? What was Tash doing?

At last her sister reappeared, flushed in the face. Without speaking, she bent to snap Pa's brakes off, and spun the wheelchair so savagely that Pa protested.

'What's happening? Where are you going?' Clancy trotted after them in alarm as Tash thrust the chair along the concourse.

'Country trains leave from a different station,' said Tash shortly.

'What station?'

'Back there. The one we walked past on the way here.'

'So we have to walk all the way back?'

'Yep.'

'Bugger!' said Pa, when he understood what was happening.

Clancy had to jog to keep up. 'So – we're still going, though?'

'Of course! Why wouldn't we?'

Clancy fell back, realising that Tash was not just furious, she was also embarrassed. How could she have made a mistake like that? Tash never made mistakes. Clancy was used to her older sister knowing everything about everything. No wonder Tash felt humiliated.

Clancy guessed that now would not be a good time to remind Tash about her blisters. Or to ask if they could have caught a train to the other station, instead of walking all the way.

Pa let out a sudden shout.

'What now?' Tash was so cross, she even snapped at Pa. 'You can't need the toilet again, you've only just gone.'

Pa's arm shot up and Clancy and Tash tipped back their heads to look.

'I can't see anything,' grumbled Tash.

'Sp! Sp!' Pa's hand traced a path above their heads.

High in the cloudless sky, wheeling level with the tower-tops, a hawk soared above the city. Far above the dust and noise, riding on the currents, a silent visitor from another time, a time before cities and skyscrapers and cars, a time of endless plains and boundless forests. The hawk banked, and slid out of sight.

Clancy let out a long breath she hadn't realised she was holding. She was fairly sure that the hawk hadn't been sent by Nan; but it still felt like a good omen, a blessing.

'Sp-sp-sp,' Pa reminded Tash.

'Oh, yeah.' Tash turned to Clancy. 'Pa showed me this article the other day about peregrine falcons nesting in the city. On a window ledge, on the thirty-fifth floor. I guess to them, it's the same as a cliff.'

'Wow, that's so cool.'

Clancy hugged the image of that hawk inside herself as they trudged on. It was so proud, so free and wild and strong, riding on the back of the wind. If Tash was a bird, she would probably be a hawk. And what kind of bird would Clancy herself be? Probably a puffin, she decided gloomily. No one could take a puffin seriously, waddling around with their ridiculous big feet and noses. Yes, Clancy was sure she'd be a puffin.

And Pa? Perhaps a seagull, with snowy white feathers, a harsh call, and a broken wing...And Nan would have to be a shearwater, swooping alone above the ocean all day, but cruising in to the shore at nightfall to check on her family...

Lost in her thoughts, Clancy bumped into Tash's back as she and Pa halted at the traffic lights. 'Watch it!'

'Sorry—' Clancy gaped as they crossed the road, noticing the name of the railway station on the huge sign spanning the concourse. 'Tash! Look! It's called Southern Cross!'

'Yeah, so?'

'It's the name of a constellation. Stars! Don't you get it? It's Nan again. It's a sign from Nan.'

'It's just the name of the station,' said Tash. 'It's been the name of this station for years and years. Nothing to do with Nan.'

But Clancy was content. She knew they were on the right path again.

The enormous, drafty cavern of the station had a high, wavy roof like frozen surf. It smelled of diesel and echoed with the roar of engines, the squeal of brakes, and muffled announcements that managed to be noisy and incomprehensible at the same time. Pa rubbed the dust from his watering eyes.

'Can I have a drink?' said Clancy. 'And I still need Band-Aids for my blisters. I've got them on both feet now.'

'You're not the only one in pain,' said Tash. 'My arm muscles are killing me.' She pulled some coins from her pocket and pointed. 'There's a vending machine. You get us all some drinks while I find out about the train.'

'What if there isn't one? What if we've missed it?'

Tash threw her an exasperated look. 'You are so *defeatist*. At least let me check. You can get me an apple juice.'

Clancy hung back. 'Can't you do it?'

'Do I have to do *everything*?'

But Tash stomped off to buy the drinks, thrust two bottles into Clancy's hands, and then marched off to investigate the train situation.

There was nowhere to sit down.

'You're lucky, Pa – at least you've got your own chair.'

'Sp-sp,' he agreed smugly.

Clancy eyed the concrete floor but decided it was too dirty to sit on. Anyway, someone would tell her off, maybe throw them out of the station, maybe report them to the police. She'd almost forgotten that the police were hunting for them...Glancing around warily, she spied a pair of uniformed officers strolling down the stairs from the upper level. With a gasp, she hastily wheeled Pa behind an advertising billboard.

'Sp-sp!' said Pa indignantly; he'd spilled his drink down his shirt.

'Sorry, sorry,' whispered Clancy, peeping out. 'It's okay – they're gone.'

Suddenly she felt super self-conscious. If she and Tash had been on their own, they could have blended in with the crowds easily. But two teenage girls with an old man in a wheelchair? Not so much.

'Hello there, sir. Everything okay?'

Clancy jumped. She had been so busy looking out for the police that she hadn't seen the two security officers approaching from the other direction.

'Sp-sp-sp?' Pa looked from the officers to Clancy and back again.

'Sorry, sir. Didn't quite catch that?'

Clancy clutched the handles tightly and tried to hide behind the wheelchair.

'Sp-sp-sp!' Pa pointed at Clancy.

The officer looked at her. 'Is he okay?'

'Yes,' whispered Clancy. 'He can't – he had a stroke. He can't talk.'

'Oh, right. Sorry to hear that. Everything okay with you guys? You looked like you were hiding from someone, tucked away behind here.'

The officer was smiling amiably, but Clancy had the feeling the question was serious. She nodded vigorously, and looked around in desperation for Tash. Why hadn't she come back?

'So—' said the officer, after a pause. 'Yes, you're hiding? Or yes, you're okay?'

'We're okay.' Clancy tried to speak more loudly.

'You waiting for someone? Is an adult with you?'

'My sister's coming back in a minute,' said Clancy.

'Mind if we have a quick word with her?'

'Here she is!' cried Clancy in relief.

Tash walked up, scowling. 'What's going on? Everything okay?'

'Just what we were wondering,' said the officer. 'You're the sister, are you?'

'Yes.'

'You waiting to meet someone? Or going somewhere?'

'Sorry,' said Tash, 'have we done anything wrong? Are we breaking some law by standing here? Because I don't think it's really any of your business what we do with our grandfather.'

'He's your granddad, is he?'

'Yes.'

'Sp-sp-sp!' said Pa.

'Okay,' said the officer. 'No need to get excited. Got any ID I could take a look at, sir?'

'You know what?' said Tash. 'We've got a train to catch. We haven't really got time for this.'

'So you are going somewhere?'

'We're going to visit our aunt,' whispered Clancy.

'We've got tickets. Look.' Tash brandished three tickets then shoved them back in her pocket. 'Happy now?'

'Hey,' said the officer. 'Let's keep it polite, okay? How about that ID?'

'We haven't got any,' said Tash.

'Driver's licence? Pension card? Nothing?'

'He lives in an old people's home. He doesn't need any of that.'

'He's like the Queen,' said Clancy.

They all turned to stare at her as if she were crazy.

'The Queen doesn't have a driver's licence either,' said Clancy feebly.

'We're going to miss our train,' said Tash, elbowing her sister aside to grasp the handles of the wheelchair. 'So unless you've got an actual reason to keep us here…'

Reluctantly the officers stood aside to let them pass. Clancy glanced back fearfully as Tash pushed Pa along the concourse, and saw one of them talking into a radio clipped to his jacket.

'I think they're checking on us, Tash. Maybe the police are telling them that we're wanted for kidnapping, and breaking and entering, and assault with a wheelchair. Maybe they're going to come after us—' Clancy squealed. 'They're walking this way, Tash!'

Tash swore, and broke into a trot, trundling Pa faster and faster along the concourse. 'This platform – quick, this is our train.'

Clancy dragged open the door and Tash manoeuvred Pa inside with a thump. 'Are they coming? Did they see us?'

Clancy leaned out. She couldn't see the security officers on the platform, but maybe that meant they'd already climbed on board the train. Anxiously she peered through the glass doors into the next carriage. There was no sign of the officers there either, but Clancy didn't feel safe to sit down and relax until the train lurched forward, then began to glide out of the station, slowly at first but then picking up speed, heading west.

23

The air-conditioned train was so chilly that Tash pulled her hoodie out of her backpack and put it on. She parked Pa in the space reserved for bicycles, prams and wheelchairs. He shifted fretfully in his seat and complained, 'Sp-sp-sp.'

'A drink? The toilet? Are you cold?'

'He doesn't have a cardigan or anything,' worried Clancy.

Pa shook his head impatiently. 'Nah, nah.' He sniffed his armpit and grimaced.

'You are getting a bit stinky,' agreed Tash. 'When we get to Bee's place, she can wash your shirt.'

Clancy glanced down at her own grubby T-shirt. 'Chuck in our stuff while she's at it.'

'Speak for yourself.' Tash pulled a deodorant from her bag and flourished it smugly. 'Some of us are still quite fragrant, thank you.'

That reminded Clancy of Nan's perfume, and she sniffed hopefully. But there was no scent of lily-of-the-valley. Tash snapped, 'For God's sake, blow your nose!'

Clancy stopped sniffing and turned her attention to the view through the window as the suburbs rolled past, with abandoned factories and half-built apartment blocks, rows of hundred-year-old terrace cottages and the feathery treetops of hidden parks. A golden pagoda appeared on the horizon, its roof dazzling in the midday sun. 'Wow, what's that?'

'A temple, I guess. I could look it up if I had my phone.'

Clancy couldn't think of anything witty to say. How did Tash always manage to pull out a perfect put-down? Instead, Clancy poked out her tongue.

'Mature,' said Tash. 'Impressive.'

The temple slid out of sight and the train crossed a wide, sleepy river. The factories and houses slipped away, and before long the train was racing though flat yellow paddocks dotted with black and white cows and sprinkled with sheep. Here and there a dead tree stood out against the sky like a majestic sculpture.

Tash gave her sister a nudge. 'Pa's asleep.'

Pa's head drooped on his chest, and his eyes were closed. His scalp, pink from the sun, showed through his feathery white hair like the skin of a baby mouse. His chair rocked gently with the swaying of the train.

'Tash?' murmured Clancy. 'You know how everyone's after us...do you think we should take him back?'

'To The Elms? No way!' whispered Tash fiercely. 'If we take him back there, I think he'll *die*. Like a bird in captivity.'

'Literally die?' Clancy was shocked.

'We're taking him to Bee's. We promised. We can't turn round now.'

Clancy swallowed. 'I wish Mum and Dad were here.'

'Well, they're not,' snapped Tash. 'We have to do it ourselves. There's just us.'

And Nan, thought Clancy. But unless you counted the name of the station, there hadn't been much sign of Nan's guidance this morning. Even the daytime moon had disappeared.

Clancy stared down at the floor, and a lump rose in her throat. Then, unexpectedly, Tash put an arm around her shoulders and squeezed. Tash didn't do hugs, except on the footy field. Clancy was so surprised she nearly fell off her seat.

'We'll be all right, peanut,' said Tash gruffly. 'But *don't cry*.'

Clancy rubbed her eyes with the back of her hand, and swallowed. 'Okay,' she said in a small voice.

'Do you want your book?'

'Yes, please.'

The books were definitely real, thought Clancy, as she turned hers over in her hands. So maybe the arcade was still there. Otherwise, time travel was the only possible explanation. If the bookshop *had* gone, where was Antonia now? Clancy hoped she was strolling along a beach somewhere with her friend Verity. And was

Antonia the one who'd worked the magic, or Nan? If it was magic. Clancy would never know...

She sighed, and opened her book. Soon she was lost in the Aboriginal stories of the stars: the seven sisters being chased across the Western Desert before escaping into the sky as the Pleiades; the Yolngu story about three brothers fishing from their canoe, more familiar to Clancy as the stars of Orion; about the emu in the sky, a constellation of dark spaces spread out across the bright backdrop of the Milky Way in Gomeroi country; and Barnumbirr, the Morning Star, who rises before dawn, drawing behind her a rope of light along which Yolngu people are able to communicate with their ancestors. Clancy's heart skipped a beat. Carefully she read the story again. Was Nan's spirit using that rope of light to send messages to her?

Clancy wasn't a fan of ghost stories; she'd always been terrified of the idea of lurking malevolent presences in the night. Ghosts were supposed to be transparent, or dressed in white, and they were meant to glide silently down dark corridors and make the air turn cold. They weren't supposed to laugh gently and leave star clues and smell like lily-of-the-valley.

But maybe Australian ghosts were different. Maybe Nan was different. The thought of Nan's spirit hovering nearby was comforting, not frightening. Even if Clancy couldn't see her, she liked to think she was still there... the way the light of a star was still there, behind the sun's light...

Clancy drowsed, rocked by the rhythm of the train, her forehead resting against the glass. She woke with a start at the sound of Pa's low, grumbling voice as he fidgeted in his chair. Tash's head was nodding, her eyes were shut. A shot of panic jolted through Clancy: what if they'd missed Quoll Creek? What if they'd travelled straight across the desert, all the way to Perth? *Nan wouldn't let us do that,* she thought. *She'd wake me up in time.* Her panic subsided.

'Plan B,' she murmured, and chuckled to herself.

'What?' Tash's eyes flicked open. 'Did you say something? Are we there?'

Clancy shook her head. 'Plan B. That was all. This is Plan B. Bee for Beatrice.'

'That's not bad, peanut,' said Tash.

Clancy glowed. 'Thanks.'

The yellow paddocks were behind them now, and the train was rushing through wooded hills, crossing narrow creeks and rushing past grey-green trees. Clancy could see holes dug into in the hillside, overgrown with brambles and bush. Alex had said this was gold rush country. Perhaps there were caves and tunnels still out there, hiding secret veins of gold in the darkness, like Pa's treasure had been hidden under the Rosella house. Perhaps Bee had found gold. A gigantic nugget, big enough to pay for a whole farm with lambs and chickens and kittens, and a full-time nurse for Pa...

'Ah!' Pa gave a sudden cry, and Clancy jumped.

The train was slowing down, and an announcement crackled over the PA. *The next station is Quoll Creek.*

'We're here!' cried Clancy.

Tash leapt up, slinging the backpack onto her shoulder. 'I'll get Pa, you grab the door.'

With an excruciating squeal of brakes, the train slowed to a halt. Clancy jabbed at the button on the door until it slid open.

'How's the gap?' demanded Tash.

'Not too bad.'

Expertly Tash spun the wheelchair to ease Pa through the doorway. They'd learned by now that it was best to take steps and gaps backward wherever possible, so Pa wouldn't tip out. 'Hey, hey!' protested Pa as the chair jolted onto the platform.

Clancy gasped. 'My book!'

'*Jeez*, Clancy!' Tash let go of the wheelchair, jumped back onto the train, and darted to where she and Clancy had been sitting.

'Tash, *quick*!' shrieked Clancy.

'Sp-sp-sp!' Pa shouted. The wheelchair was slowly rolling down the platform.

Clancy raced after him and grabbed the handles. 'I've got you.'

'Phew!' Pa mopped his forehead, and thrust out his hand toward Tash, visible through the window of the train. 'Sp-sp-sp?'

'Come on, Tash!' yelled Clancy.

A whistle blew, warning signals beeped. Tash dipped out of sight, bobbed up and sprinted to the end of the carriage. She jammed her foot in the door just as it was closing.

Clancy screamed, '*Tash*!'

Just in time, Tash managed to force the doors apart and hurl herself out onto the platform. Someone on the train yelled at her and she jauntily showed them her finger as the train roared out of the station.

Clancy's knees were shaking. She clutched at the handles of Pa's chair for support as Tash strolled up and thrust the book of star stories at her. 'Do you want this? Or should I look after it?'

Clancy pressed the book to her chest. 'No! I mean, I want it. I've got it.'

Tash shrugged. 'It's just, you know, first the phone, now the book... You've still got those photos of Nan, right? And Bee's address? Or have you lost them, too?'

Clancy's hand flew to her shorts pocket. But the envelope was still there, safe and sound. '*No*! They're *fine*!'

'Okay. Chill.' Buoyed by the triumph of escaping from the train, and perhaps also by her success in upsetting her sister, Tash gave her smuggest, most irritating smile.

24

But Tash wasn't smiling for long. A railway employee, a stocky, red-faced woman in a dark uniform, came hurrying up to them.

'That was extremely dangerous, jumping out of a moving train. If I decided to report you, you'd have to pay a fine.'

'It wasn't even moving yet!' Tash was on a high, flushed and ready for a fight.

The railway woman looked the three of them up and down. 'On your own, are you? Someone coming to pick you up?'

Clancy groaned inwardly. Not this again!

Tash said, 'We're not on our own. This is our grandfather.'

The woman folded her arms. 'You don't look related.' She leaned over, right in to Pa's face. 'Do. You. Know. These. Kids?'

Pa stared at her, mystified. 'What?'

'He's our *grandfather*,' said Tash. She didn't actually

add *you idiot*, but the words were clearly implied. She started to wheel Pa away.

But Clancy almost sympathised with the woman for being suspicious; they did all look pretty feral. She and Tash were sweaty and bedraggled, Pa had a stain on his shirt, and Clancy had spilled half a cup of cold coffee over her shorts while they were cleaning up Alex's flat.

The woman held up a hand. 'Hold on a minute. I want to hear it from the gentleman himself.' She planted herself solidly in front of the wheelchair. 'Excuse me, sir. Are these really your grandchildren? Adopted, are they?'

Pa stared at her in bewilderment. 'Nah, nah. Yeah, no.'

Clancy and Tash exchanged a glance. *Uh-oh*.

'He's had a stroke,' said Tash. 'You have to be really clear with your questions. He sometimes gets *yes* and *no* mixed up.' She knelt to peer into Pa's worried, confused face. 'Pa? This – lady – wants to know if me and Clancy are your family. We are, aren't we?'

'Yes!' Pa glared at the woman and clenched his fist.

She raised her hands and stepped back. 'Okay, okay, no drama.'

But when Clancy looked back as they left the station, she was still watching them.

'Interfering b— busybody,' muttered Tash.

'Pfft!' said Pa.

Quoll Creek was an old goldfields town. The broad main street was lined with terrace cottages, and shops selling boiled lollies and lace and patchwork quilts to tourists.

'Sp-sp-sp,' groaned Pa suddenly.

'Toilet?' chorused Clancy and Tash, who both recognised the signals by now.

Tash marched the wheelchair swiftly along the street, scanning for cafés without steps, or a pub that might have a disabled toilet inside. Pa was wincing and clutching the arm of the chair by the time they finally found a toilet in a courtyard. A sign on the door read *Patrons of the Neptune Café only*.

'Neptune!' cried Clancy. 'It's a sign!'

Tash ignored her. 'Go and get the key. Quick, Clance!'

Clancy's delight turned to horror. 'Go to the café?'

'Yes! Quick!'

'Ask them for the toilet key?'

'Yes! And hurry! Do you want Pa to wet his pants in the street?'

'Can't you go?' But when Clancy saw the expression on her sister's face, she turned and fled from the courtyard, back onto the street. Frantically she swivelled left and right, ran a little way up the street then down again.

'You right? Lost someone?'

Clancy jumped, though the voice was friendly. A tall, gangling teenage boy with curling dark hair, pale skin and high cheekbones was smiling down at her.

'I'm okay,' squeaked Clancy. 'But – do you know where the Neptune Café is?'

'Just up there.'

As the boy pointed, Clancy noticed an oversized wooden tag dangling from his hand, with a blue planet painted on it...

'Is that the toilet key?' she gasped.

'Yeah, it is. You need it?'

The boy tossed it over and by some miracle of hand-eye coordination, Clancy managed to catch it. 'Thank you!' She sprinted back to where Tash and Pa were waiting.

Tash grabbed the key. 'Did you have to buy something?'

'No – anyway, I don't have any money.'

'Never mind, tell me later.' Tash was already pushing Pa toward the toilet, and after a brief fumble with the key, they vanished inside.

Relieved, Clancy turned around, and let out a yelp as she collided with the curly-haired boy.

'Sorry,' he said. 'I just thought I should wait till you're done, and then I could show you where the café is.'

'Oh, yeah, you're right. I didn't think of that.'

There was a brief, awkward silence. At least, it felt awkward for Clancy. The boy didn't seem worried at all.

'I didn't need the key for me,' said Clancy after a moment. 'It was for my grandfather.'

'Yeah, I saw.'

'He's had a stroke. He needs some help with – everything.' Clancy felt her face flushing. 'That's why my sister went in with him...'

'Yep, that makes sense.'

'So...I'll just wait for them to come out,' explained Clancy. *Oh help*. Could she possibly sound any more pathetic? She almost wished that she was in the loo with Pa, and Tash was out here having this painful conversation. Except it wouldn't be painful for Tash. She would know exactly what to say. Clancy didn't dare look at the boy; she didn't want to see him laughing at her.

Only a few minutes had passed, but to Clancy it seemed like hours before Tash poked her head out of the bathroom door.

'Hey, Clance, can you buy us some afternoon tea? Pa's a bit grumpy, I think he might be hungry.' Tash caught sight of the boy, and gave him a cool stare. 'You right?'

Clancy wasn't sure if Tash was talking to her or him. She said, 'It's okay, Tash, he gave me the key.'

'You followed her from the café?' said Tash to the boy.

'No, no...he was in the street...I couldn't find the café...'

Tash cut through Clancy's stammers with an impatient gesture. 'Just buy us some sandwiches or something. I've put some cash in here.' Unexpectedly she threw her wallet to Clancy, who fumbled the catch. The wallet dropped to the pavement, and Tash rolled her eyes. 'Meet you there.'

'But I don't—'

It was too late; Tash had disappeared back inside the cubicle.

'—know what to buy,' mumbled Clancy.

The boy said, 'Want me to show you where the café is?'

Clancy chewed her lip. 'Okay.' After all, he probably couldn't rob and murder her in broad daylight in the main street of Quoll Creek. If she was careful.

She followed, a step behind him, as he led her along the footpath to a little café with long wooden benches and jam jars for light fittings.

'Here you go,' said the boy. 'We had the spanakopita. It was pretty good.'

Clancy nodded. *So that's how you pronounce it.* But she knew she would never dare try to order it in public. She wondered who *we* might be, and as if he'd read her mind, the boy gave a cheerful wave to a couple of women sitting at a table by the wall.

'My mums,' he said.

Clancy waved to them, too, and they waved back with slightly puzzled expressions. Embarrassed, Clancy said, 'I'd better—' She motioned to the counter.

'Yep, sure, cool.'

But they lingered in the middle of the café, fumbling for a more satisfactory way to end their encounter.

'Well...see ya,' said the boy at last.

'Thanks,' said Clancy hastily.

But by then Tash and Pa had arrived, bumping the wheelchair over the threshold, both of them looking grumpy.

'What?' said Tash. 'Haven't you bought anything yet?'

'I just got here!' With relief, Clancy tossed the wallet back to her sister. 'And I didn't know what you wanted,' she offered as a plausible excuse. '*And* you have to give the key back.'

'Huh,' said Tash. She slipped on Pa's brakes and marched to the counter, and Clancy took shelter behind the wheelchair.

While Tash was still ordering, the boy and his two mothers stood up and left the café, giving Clancy and Pa friendly smiles as they passed.

'Bye,' said the boy.

'Bye.' To her dismay, Clancy felt her face grow pink. *It doesn't matter*, she told herself fiercely. *You're never going to see him again.*

25

They took the sandwiches across the road to a park and unwrapped them at a splintery picnic table under a tree.

'Ham and salad,' said Tash.

'I *hate* ham!'

'You had your chance to pick, and you blew it,' said Tash with her mouth full. 'Just pull the ham out if you don't want it. Give it to the birds.'

There were a few pigeons hovering about hopefully, strutting on the dry grass.

'But it all tastes like ham now. It's contaminated. Cont-ham-inated.' Clancy couldn't stop herself. 'Why couldn't we go straight to Bee's and use her toilet, and then we could have had something good for lunch at her place.'

'Pa couldn't wait, could you, Pa?'

Pa didn't answer. He was chewing gingerly; then he spat a mouthful back into the bag, screwed it up and shoved it away.

'See, Pa thinks they're gross, too!' said Clancy triumphantly.

'God, you guys are so ungrateful! I swear, I'm almost starting to see where Mum and Dad are coming from when they say that.' Tash scrambled up and brushed crumbs from her lap.

'Where is Bee's place, anyway?'

'I've got the address, but I don't know how to get there,' admitted Tash. 'I could have looked it up, if only I had my phone. I don't know how far it is. It might be just a short walk, or it could be a long taxi ride. Except I can't call a taxi either, without my phone…'

A thought popped into Clancy's mind before she could stop it. *I bet that boy would lend us his phone.*

And then a second thought: *I bet Nan could arrange for us to bump into him again…Nan? Could you? Please?* Casually she gazed around in all directions: to the shops, the parked cars, the scattering of pedestrians strolling along the footpath. Her heart gave a sudden thump. There he was – climbing into a long, low car with his two mothers. He was getting into the driver's seat; there was a yellow learner's plate stuck to the back window. So he must be at least sixteen…

As she watched, he carefully edged the car backward, then pulled out onto the road. They were driving away. It was too late; they'd gone.

Nan had set up a chance for her, and she'd missed it. Clancy swallowed hard, and looked away.

'We'll try the lace shop,' Tash was saying. 'That looks the most harmless-est.'

'Not a word,' murmured Clancy; but she followed.

Inside the shop, they found a tiny, twinkling-eyed woman dressed in what looked like an old tablecloth.

'Excuse me,' said Tash with her most brilliant smile. 'Do you have a number for a taxi?'

'A *taxi*, darling?' It was as if Tash had asked for an elephant.

'Yes, please. A maxi-taxi. You know, to fit a wheel-chair.'

'You mean one of those van things? We don't have any of those around here.' She squinted doubtfully. 'I suppose you could try ordering one from Dunkley?'

Clancy was tired. She would have been happy to wait in the cool of the lace shop for as long as it took, but Tash was impatient. 'That's okay, we'll walk. Can you tell us how to get to Ginger Gully Road?'

The woman pursed her lips. 'Hm, that's quite a hike, darling.'

Tash squared her shoulders. 'We can do it.'

'Well, if you're sure…Just follow this road. That direction.' She pointed. 'There's a sign at the turn-off. You can't miss it.'

'Cool, thanks.' Tash wheeled Pa out of the shop and Clancy followed.

'Pa's thirsty.' Clancy had no idea if Pa was thirsty or not, but she figured this would be a safer way of making

Tash buy drinks for them all, rather than asking for one for herself.

Tash let out an exaggerated sigh, but she went into a supermarket while Pa and Clancy waited outside. Clancy was just realising she'd forgotten to ask for Band-Aids, when her sister came out again with three bottles of water.

'Sp-sp-sp!' complained Pa, struggling to unscrew the cap with one hand.

Clancy undid it for him, and trudged along behind Tash as she pushed Pa past the row of shops and a small wooden school building, past a grander house with verandahs and a lush garden, past a church and a tiny graveyard. When the footpath came to an end, Tash glanced left and right, then wheeled Pa down onto the smooth bitumen.

'Tash! You can't walk on the *road*!'

'Sp-sp-sp,' grumbled Pa.

'Lighten up. We did it at Rosella. There's no traffic. No footpath either. Where are we supposed to walk?'

'I guess,' said Clancy glumly. But she plodded as close to the edge as she could, so if anyone accused her of walking on the road, at least she could say she was trying not to break the law.

'See?' said Tash after ten minutes. 'No cars.'

'Huh?' Clancy looked at her sister in surprise. She wasn't thinking about traffic at all; she'd just spotted the dim disc of Nan's moon, hanging in the sky just in front of them, like a pale lantern showing them the way.

26

The sun was slipping down the sky and the light was turning bronze when they reached the edge of the forest and the turn-off for Ginger Gully Road.

'At least it'll be shady now.' Tash wiped her face, damp with sweat, on her sleeve.

The road wound away down a gentle hill, through grey-green trees with thin pale trunks and a dense under-growth of bracken and ferns.

'Sp-sp-sp,' grumbled Pa, shifting in his chair.

'Are you positive this is the right road, Tash? I can't see any houses.'

'There could be hundreds of houses in there, hidden in the trees. This is definitely Ginger Gully Road, and Bee's house is number five hundred and forty-six.'

'*Five hundred and forty-six*? Are you *serious*? If this end starts at number one, it's going to be *miles* away. I thought we must be nearly there, and now you tell me it's *five hundred and forty-six*?'

'We are nearly there. We must be. It's different in the country.'

But Tash didn't sound as confident as usual.

'Sp-sp-sp?' Pa gestured back toward the town.

'No! We're not going back now!'

Tash seized the handles and began to push the wheelchair along the rough road. Well, if Tash was going to keep pushing, Clancy supposed she'd have to follow, though she was hot and tired and the blisters on her heels were squidging with blood. It was fine for Pa; all he had to do was sit there.

One foot after the other. All Clancy wanted now was to find their aunt and hand over Pa to her. They were so close now, and the moon and the Neptune Café were signs they were on the right track. But once Bee had taken charge… Then what? There would be no Tim and Harriet and Bruno to go home to. Just an empty, lifeless apartment wondering why its family had abandoned it…

'Clancy, you're not crying *again*, are you?'

'I'm not,' gulped Clancy. 'And FYI, I've only cried *once*.'

'Yeah, right. Whatever.' Tash sounded too weary to argue with her. Slowly she pushed Pa along the old, cracked bitumen. The trees closed around them, cool and hushed and shady. Clancy remembered all the films and television shows she'd ever seen about wild animals and bushrangers who lurked in forests, and aliens who crash-landed their ships in the wilderness. She trod on Tash's heels.

'Watch it!'

'Sorry.'

The bitumen petered out into a red gravelly track, pocked with potholes and scored with wheel ruts. They struggled on, more and more slowly, as the sun filtered through the leaves, making leopard-spots of light and shade on the path. The track snaked up and down hills, and even with Clancy's help, it was tough work to move the wheelchair.

Tash stopped to take a swig of water. 'Have you put on weight, Pa?'

'Sp-sp,' Pa grumbled.

'Well, we can't *go* any faster.'

Pa made as if to get up and walk, but Clancy and Tash were too tired and hot to even pretend to laugh.

'My turn,' said Clancy bravely, and Tash stood back to let her push. But though she heaved and strained with all her might, Clancy couldn't make the wheelchair budge.

'Hey!' she said, examining the wheel. 'Pa's got a flat tyre.'

'Yeah, right. Any excuse.'

'I'm not joking. Look.'

The left tyre was flat as a Mexican wrap. Tash yelled out a swearword.

'You must have run over a piece of broken glass, or a nail or something,' said Clancy.

'Oh, ya think?'

Tash squatted by the path, pulled out her ponytail and retied it, her face screwed up in thought. She retied her hair again, and then a third time. Clancy waited. Tash wandered up the track to scout for passing traffic; but they hadn't seen a single car since they'd turned off the main road. Clancy tipped her head back to look for Nan's moon, but the sky was screened by the trees and she couldn't see it anymore. Nan had deserted them.

Pa rubbed his bristly chin and said, 'Hm...'

Which wasn't a helpful contribution either, but Clancy noticed that Tash didn't tell *him* off.

'Okay,' said Tash at last. 'We can't keep pushing the wheelchair with a flat tyre. A: it's really impossible to do; and B: it might damage the wheels.' She looked at Clancy. 'One of us has to go and find Bee and bring her back with a car to pick up Pa.'

There was a pause.

'Well, I can't go,' said Clancy.

'Why not?'

Clancy began to panic. 'I don't know where her house is! I don't know what to say to her! I can't talk to people!'

'It's not "people", it's just Bee. You know Bee.'

'I haven't seen her for, you know, *ever*? I'm not going. You can't make me.'

Tash folded her arms. 'Cool, cool, cool. So you'll wait here with Pa? While it gets dark. And you'll be fine if he

166

needs the toilet. Or if a car comes past with a murderer inside.'

Clancy was silent.

'Off you go then,' said Tash. 'Number five hundred and forty-six. Better hurry.'

Clancy muttered, 'I said I don't want to.'

'What's that?'

'No!' shouted Clancy. 'I said no! I'm not going!'

Tash's fists were on her hips. 'Yes, you are.'

'No! I'm sick of you ordering me around. I'm leaving. I'm going home.'

Clancy turned and began to stomp back along the red dirt track toward Quoll Creek. She was so angry that she could hardly see. She stumbled over the ruts and dips in the road, sweat stinging her eyes. She could hear Tash calling, but she didn't turn around.

There was a pounding of feet along the track, and suddenly Tash was there, grabbing at her sister's shoulder. 'Clancy! Wait!'

'Leave me alone! I hate you!'

'Don't – Clance, don't go.'

Clancy set her jaw and stared into the trees.

'Please. *Please*. Clance, I need you. You can't go. I can't do this without you.'

Clancy chewed her cheek.

'Pa's upset,' pleaded Tash. 'He wants you to come back. He doesn't understand. He tried to wheel himself after you...'

Clancy took an involuntary step back in Pa's direction, then stopped herself. She stared down at the red dirt. There was silence.

'I'm sorry, all right?' said Tash at last. 'I thought you liked me being in charge.'

'Mostly I do,' mumbled Clancy. 'Just not all the time.' Their eyes met.

'I mean it,' said Tash threateningly. 'I really need you.'

Clancy thrust her hands into the pockets of her shorts. One hand curled around the envelope with the photographs of Nan. She drew in a deep breath. 'Okay,' she said. 'I'll go. I'll do it.'

Tash blew out a sigh of relief. 'Thanks, Clancy.'

Was that all she'd wanted, just a simple *thank you*? But somehow the words made Clancy feel included, as if she were a full partner in this quest, instead of someone just tagging along, a satellite helplessly circling Planet Tash.

Hand in hand, the sisters jogged back to where Pa was sitting.

'Ah!' he sighed, when he saw them coming.

'Help me get him off the road before you go,' said Tash. 'In case a car does come.'

Together they heaved and pulled and pushed and managed to shift the wheelchair across the gravel and into the bracken at the side of the track. 'Bugger!' shouted Pa as the chair lurched suddenly, then stuck, listing sideways, one wheel trapped in the ditch none of them had noticed. 'Ah, no, no, no!'

Tash swore, a yell of frustration, a worse word than last time. The two girls hauled and shoved, but they couldn't free the chair.

'Just go!' panted Tash at last. 'Run!'

'Sorry, Pa!' wailed Clancy. She began to run down the track, skidded to a halt, then ran back, dropped a kiss on the top of Pa's feathery head, then ran off again. At the next bend in the road, she turned to wave. Tash and Pa waved back. But then the trees swallowed them up, and she couldn't see them anymore.

27

Clancy stumbled along the track, her eyes darting from side to side so she wouldn't miss a signpost or a mailbox or a house, something that might tell her how close she was to Bee's, or a signal from Nan – a star carved into the trunk of a tree, like there had been at Rosella, or a moon-shaped stone. At this point, she'd take anything.

Nan? Are you there?

The sun slanted low through the leaves. She wished she had a watch. She wished she'd brought her water bottle. What if she couldn't find Bee's house? How far should she go before she turned back? Part of her longed to turn around already, but she couldn't face Tash's anger, or Pa's disappointment. She slipped her hand into her pocket and touched the envelope of photographs for reassurance. *Go on*, said an encouraging voice inside her head. Or was it the chime of a bird from deep among the trees? *Go on, go on!*

Clancy went on.

But then a movement in the undergrowth caught her eye. She stopped, frozen. A pair of dark eyes stared back at her. *Nan?* Clancy held her breath, her heart knocking.

A face swam into focus around the dark, solemn eyes: a furred grey mask, a dark muzzle. Clancy burst out laughing with relief, with disappointment. It was just a kangaroo, about ten metres away, gazing gravely at her across the curling bracken.

For a long moment Clancy and the kangaroo stared at each other. Its face seemed so kindly, so wise, so gentle. For a second Clancy had a wild fantasy that it might lead her to Bee, like a magic animal in a story. Tentatively she held out her hand toward it.

The kangaroo's ears twitched, its head turned, and before Clancy's hand had dropped, it gathered itself and bounded silently away, leaping through the ferns and across a clearing between the trees, and vanished.

Clancy let out a long, trembling breath. Was this a sign from Nan? Was she supposed to follow? Kangaroos didn't have anything to do with the stars or the moon. If it had been an emu, then maybe...

Squinting across the clearing, she glimpsed a cottage in a paddock, on the side of a hill, a little farm house just like the one she'd imagined. But it was so far off the road, surely it couldn't be Bee's place. It didn't look as if it belonged to Ginger Gully Road at all.

As she stood there hesitating, the bird call chimed again, from further down the track. *Go on, go on!*

Maybe the kangaroo didn't have anything to do with anything, Clancy told herself sensibly. Maybe it was just a kangaroo. Wasn't that amazing enough, to have had a close encounter with a kangaroo, without bringing ghosts and magic into it? And Pa and Tash were waiting.

She hurried on along the path, through the afternoon light that seemed to be gradually thickening, like golden syrup dripping from the trees.

Dripping...dripping...Clancy became uncomfortably aware that she needed the toilet. Once she'd allowed the thought to surface, she knew she was busting; she couldn't hold on any longer. She stumbled off the track until she was waist-deep in bracken, fumbled with her shorts, squatted down and let go. The relief was exquisite.

She mopped herself up as best she could manage with a handful of grass and pulled up her pants, wiping her hands on her shorts and making sure Nan's photographs hadn't fallen out of her pocket. She promised herself that she'd wash her hands as soon as she got to Bee's...

...as soon as she got back onto the track...

With a stab of panic, Clancy realised she'd lost her bearings. She was standing in a sea of bracken, surrounded by trees in all directions, endless trees, as many trees as stars in the sky; she was absolutely alone, and she couldn't see the path anywhere. A kookaburra's sudden peal of laughter above her head made her jump. Slowly Clancy revolved, scanning for the path. This was how people got lost in the bush, wandering in circles, never to be seen again—

Look up, Clancy. Look up!

It was Nan's voice, soft and clear. Clancy whipped around. Was that a shadow of a figure, moving in the bracken? Or just another a kangaroo?

Look up.

She looked up, and a shaft of sunlight made her blink. The sun. The Sun, that huge star, had been shining on her right cheek. If she walked back toward the sun, she'd find the path. Clancy stumbled through the bracken, the fronds scratching her arms and bare legs. And there was the road, just where she'd left it.

She hardly felt her blisters as she sped along the track, the sun obediently glinting in the corner of her right eye. The wave of relief carried her straight past the tin sign nailed to the tree; she had to turn around and run back to double-check it.

Quoll Crk Ashram
546 GG Rd
Hari Om!

The battered sign was half painted with an elaborate, colourful circular symbol, with a smaller, swirly flourish in one corner. Clancy stared at it uncertainly. It was definitely the right address; she'd pulled the envelope out of her pocket to check. A dirt track, no more than two wheel ruts wide, turned off the red gravel road. It must be Bee's driveway.

What would Tash do?

There was only one answer.

28

Clancy hurried down the driveway. The track twisted and turned between the trees. Why would anyone need such a long driveway? Where was Bee's house?

At last she glimpsed a glint of silver through the bush, the gleam of a tin roof, and a few moments later she emerged from the trees into a car park filled with vehicles, with a low cluster of buildings beyond.

Clancy took two steps forward, then stopped. This didn't look like someone's house, or even a farm. It looked like a school camp, or maybe some kind of hotel. Was Bee working at a hotel now?

Clancy's unwilling feet carried her slowly across the car park until she saw a sign.

Reception

Hari Om

Those mysterious words again. What did they mean? Was it a spell? And there was the circular symbol, too; it was the kind of pattern that she'd seen in those calming adult colouring books. And the swirly symbol

was there again, in the bottom corner, like a signature...
An arrow pointed to the nearest of the low buildings,
which looked as if it had been moulded from caramel
mud. *Please remove your shoes* requested another sign
by the wooden double doors, and Clancy obediently
(and with relief) kicked off her runners, pushed open the
doors and tiptoed into an empty foyer area. A second,
single glass door opposite led into a courtyard garden,
surrounded on three sides by single storey buildings.

So far, despite all the cars, Clancy hadn't seen
any people. Fear gripped her gut. If this were a horror
movie, then a pile of bloodied bodies would wait around
a corner, along with a killer lurking with a butcher's
knife.

Relax! she told herself sternly. *Nan wouldn't lead you
into something like that.*

There was no one behind the reception counter.
Clancy's hand hovered over the bell. If she rang it,
someone would come – but what would she say to them?

That's the whole reason you're here! said Tash's exasperated voice inside her head.

I'll just ask for Bee, Clancy decided, and without
giving herself any more time to be scared, she banged her
hand down on the bell.

The noise jangled out into the empty space. As the
sound faded, Clancy became aware of other sounds in
the background: a distant chime, a faint murmur of
chanting. So there were people alive here somewhere.

Clancy tapped the bell again, more timidly this time, but it was less than a minute before the far door opened and someone came bustling in: a small, tanned woman, with close-cropped grey hair, about Harriet's age, dressed in long orange robes and wooden beads. Clancy gaped.

'Hari om, welcome!' said the woman. 'Havan has already started – well, it's almost finished, actually, but you're still welcome to join us.'

'I— No, I don't—' stammered Clancy.

The woman frowned. 'Are your parents here? Have you come to stay for the weekend?'

With a gasp, Clancy remembered what she was supposed to say. 'No, but my aunt is here...I think. Bee Sanderson? Is she around?'

The woman's face cleared. 'Oh, you mean Atma! She's at havan.'

'No, no, my aunt's name is Bee, Beatrice Sanderson. I need to talk to her. It's important.' A lump rose in Clancy's throat. Tash was right, she was *hopeless*, a hopeless human being. Clancy swallowed angrily.

'Just wait there. I'll get Atma for you.'

'No, it's Bee—' Clancy tried to explain, but the woman in the orange robes had already whisked herself away.

Clancy waited, shifting on the cool stone floor in her sweaty socks. She could smell them; they were putrid. Should she take them off?

She was standing on one foot, with one sock in her hand and one half-peeled off, when the orange woman returned with Bee. Clancy wobbled, staggered, and almost fell into Bee's arms. It was the shock more than the sock that unbalanced her: her aunt was bald now. Her curling hair had been completely shaven off, so that her skull was covered in dark, furry stubble, and she was wearing long robes like the orange woman's, except all in white. *It's a cult!* thought Clancy wildly. She and Tash had been counting on Bee to rescue them; were they going to have to rescue Bee instead?

'Tash? Is that you?'

'No, it's Clancy...'

'What the hell – I mean, what on *earth* are you doing here, sweetie?'

Clancy heard herself starting to babble about Pa and the flat tyre and Tash and the train and the bookshop and Polly and The Elms and the police, and it took a few minutes before Bee understood that Pa and Tash were stranded and waiting for help.

Bee pressed her hands to her cheeks. 'I'll need to borrow a car. What about the wheelchair? Can Pa get into a car?'

'I don't know. Tash got one of those maxi-taxis last time.'

They all turned their heads as the door from the court-yard creaked open, and a tall teenage boy shambled into the foyer. Clancy's mouth fell open. It was the boy from Quoll Creek, the café boy, the toilet key boy. Now *this* was a sign!

His eyes met Clancy's, and his face split into a wide grin. 'Hey!'

'Hi!'

'You two know each other?' said Bee.

'Not exactly...'

The woman in the orange robes said, 'Tom – it's Tom, isn't it?'

'Toby,' the boy corrected her amiably.

'Sorry, Toby,' amended the orange-robed woman. 'Do you think a wheelchair would fit in your mothers' car?'

'Sure,' said Toby. 'If it was folded up. And we could fold the seats down, too.'

'That would be amazing.' Bee gave him a quick, anxious smile. 'If your mother doesn't mind—'

'Mothers,' said Toby and Clancy together, and Toby grinned at her as he said, 'Two of. They'll be cool with it, for sure. Do you want me to go and pull them out of havan?'

'If you wouldn't mind,' said the orange-robed woman.

Clancy sagged back against the wall in relief. Finally, everything was coming together. This was what she'd longed for: adults to take charge. Toby returned with the two women she'd seen in the Neptune Café. There was a hurried conference with the orange-robed woman and Bee, where Toby's mums exclaimed and sympathised and seemed very happy to pick up Pa.

Clancy could smell food, and hear dishes clattering nearby. Any second now, someone would offer her dinner, and a shower – she hadn't washed her hands yet, she remembered guiltily – and then she could go to bed… Whatever this place was (some kind of weird hotel or B&B, she guessed, if people were staying for the weekend), they must have beds…It would be so nice to sleep in a bed again…

'Clancy!' Bee shook her shoulder and Clancy jumped.

'Yes, what?'

'Were you listening, sweetie? You're going with Jen and Monica to show them where Pa and Tash are.'

'But aren't you coming too?'

'I have to organise things here. This was quite a surprise, you know.' Bee's lips smiled, but her eyes looked panicky.

Clancy knew that feeling. But Bee was an adult. She should have gotten herself together by now.

'I could come along, if you like?' offered Toby.

'Oh, yes – that'd be great!' said Clancy fervently. 'Thank you!'

It was weird, though Bee was a relative and she barely knew Toby at all, it was Toby, at this moment, who felt more like a friend.

'Clancy, is it? What a great name.' One of Toby's mothers was smiling at her. 'Let's go. We don't want to keep your grandpa waiting any longer.'

Feeling Toby's presence just behind her, like some kind of guardian angel – or maybe that was taking things too far – Clancy followed the two women outside into the gathering dusk.

29

Bumping along the track. The harsh white beam of headlights cutting through the lurid coppery glow of the sinking sun. Eerie shadows flickering. Birds clamouring, chattering, shrieking, chasing through the trees. And then, high above, through a screen of leaves, an unexpected glimpse like a familiar face: the bright clear roundness of the moon. *Hello, Nan.*

Pa and Tash beside the road, so much sooner than she expected. Stumbling out of the car. Realising she hadn't put her shoes back on; the stones biting her bare feet. Pa's trembling hand grasping hers, his right foot jerking uncontrollably as it did when he was tired, his face pale beneath the grey stubble.

Toby and Jen, one on either side of Pa, levering him upright. Shuffling, half carrying him to the car. Pa collapsing into the front seat, his cry of pain and fright. Clinging to Clancy's hand.

Monica and Tash squatting by the wheelchair, trying to figure out how to fold it up. Everyone clustered around the stubborn chair, talking over each other, reaching across each other, leaving Clancy to look after Pa. His eyes squeezed shut, a tear trickling. Holding his hand, not knowing what to say.

A sudden yell, a lurch, a snap and a cheer, and the wheelchair crumples, shoved into the back of the seven-seater, everyone piles back in, doors slam shut, Clancy squashed in the back seat, separated from Tash by broad, comfortable Jen. (Toby and his mums were wearing ordinary clothes, not weird robes, which was a relief.) Fumbling with the seatbelt, giving up, guiltily, but too tired to really care. The car bumps and sways, the bodies in the back thrown against each other.

The crunch of tyres on gravel. The car stops, the doors are thrown open and people spill out – they're spilling out of the building too – and there is Bee, calling, 'Where is he? Where's my father? Is he with you? Is he okay?'

'Jeez, Bee, he's fine. Take a chill pill,' muttered Tash.

The woman in the orange robes was there, and a man with a beard, also wearing loose orange clothes. Clancy stood back, blinking with tiredness, while a crowd of people milled around, trying to extract Pa from the car. Getting him out was more difficult than putting him into it. Clancy's feet throbbed.

'Hungry?' said a low voice in her ear.

Toby loomed behind her. Mutely Clancy nodded, and she let him steer her inside, through the foyer and into one of the side rooms, where a line of people queued for food, holding plates and trays. A few wore orange robes, some yellow, some white like Bee, but many were wearing ordinary exercise gear or baggy cotton pants and tops. They were mostly women, with only a handful of men. Eerily, they were all silent. Clancy was more convinced than ever that they'd stumbled into some kind of bizarre cult – unless they all had aphasia, too? But it was too late, and she was too exhausted, to run away now. And at least Toby and his mothers seemed to be normal enough.

Clancy found herself at a table sitting next to Toby, with a plate of vegetable curry and yellow rice – more rice! – though she was too tired to eat much of it. She leaned her head on one hand. She still hadn't washed her hands, but she didn't care. She wasn't eating with her fingers. And the germs must have rubbed off by now.

After a while, Toby went away, and Bee and Tash came to sit beside her. They were talking in low, vehement voices. Clancy wished they'd go away and let her sleep…

She touched Tash's arm. 'Where's Pa?'

'Gone to bed.' Tash turned back to Bee. 'Don't worry about the money. We can pay.' She rummaged in her backpack and showed the stash of cash to her beneath the table.

Bee's mouth dropped open. 'Where did that come from?'

Heads turned in their direction. 'Ssh!' said Tash crossly. 'I'm trying to be *discreet*. It's not stolen or anything. It belongs to Pa.'

'Tashi, what have you *done*?'

'Nothing! It's what Pa wants. He *asked* to come here.'

Their voices had risen, and the orange-robed woman glided up to their table. 'Is everything all right here, Atma?'

'Yes, Jyotimitra.' Bee stood up and folded her hands. 'Perhaps you could help me explain to my niece about the ashram and what goes on here?'

'Of course. I'd be happy to help.' Jyotimitra swung one leg over the bench, sat down and gathered her robes around her with a smile.

Clancy let her head drop onto her arm. How long was this going to take?

'Hey.'

At the sound of Toby's voice, Clancy managed to drag herself upright again.

Tash said, 'We're kind of in the middle of a conversation here.'

'Nah, all good,' said Toby mildly. 'I thought Clancy might want to come to kirtan.'

Clancy shot a glance at Bee. What was he talking about? What, or where, was *keer-tan*?

'That's a good idea,' said Bee. 'You like music, don't you, sweetie?'

'I guess,' mumbled Clancy.

'Then you'll love kirtan! You wouldn't mind taking her?' That was to Toby. 'Hari om!'

'Go on, peanut,' said Tash. 'I think there's going to be an argument here, and I know how much you hate conflict.'

'I'm sure there won't be any need for conflict,' said Jyotimitra serenely.

So Clancy stumbled after Toby, out of the dining room and across the darkening courtyard. From a small pond overhung with flowering bushes came a booming, rhythmic *pobble-donk*.

'Frogs,' said Toby.

Clancy hung back. The stars of the January sky were just becoming visible, pinpricks of silver in a dark blue dome.

'Looking for anything in particular?' Toby pointed at the sky. 'That's Venus. And the Southern Cross is over there.'

'I know where the Southern Cross is,' said Clancy. 'I was trying to see the dark emu. But the Milky Way isn't clear enough.'

'We'll come out later, when it's properly dark,' said Toby. 'Then you'll see it. The sky here is amazing. You know the dark emu? So you know about stars?'

'A bit,' said Clancy.

'Cool. But we'd better go in for kirtan now.'

He held open a door into a large carpeted room, almost completely empty of furniture. Under a stained-glass window was a low platform and a scattering of musical instruments – bongos, a guitar, and something that looked like a big wooden box.

Toby lowered himself to sit cross-legged on the carpet, and Clancy, self-conscious, sat down next to him. But not too near. Other people trickled inside in twos and threes, chatting and chuckling softly, and settled themselves on the floor.

Clancy stared at the pattern in the stained glass. It was the same circular symbol that she'd seen on the signs, like an image in a kaleidoscope, a multi-pointed star, a map of a perfectly symmetrical world.

Toby noticed where she was gazing. 'That's a mandala,' he whispered. 'It's supposed to be a picture of the universe.' He shrugged to show that he didn't personally vouch for its accuracy; but Clancy didn't care if it was accurate or not. It was a star, a sign from Nan, that was the important thing. Cult or not, Nan wanted them to be here. She closed her eyes.

Her eyes were still closed when soft rhythmic tapping began from the front of the room, then a gentle strumming. But when a loud wheezing wail broke out, her eyes flew open.

The man with the beard was energetically squeezing the big wooden box, like an unwieldy accordion. It sounded like cats were being tortured.

Toby leaned across to whisper in Clancy's ear. 'Harmonium.' He wiggled his eyebrows up and down and made a discreet gagging gesture, and Clancy grinned back at him.

If she hadn't seen the mandala-star window, and if Toby hadn't been beside her, tapping his hand on his leg, she would have found what followed too peculiar for words. There was Indian-sounding music, like Sidhu had played in the Comet taxi, and there was clapping along, and chanting, and a couple of people even scrambled up to dance and play tambourines. The tempo grew faster, the music and chanting became louder and louder, until the room was almost in a frenzy. Then gradually the music slowed and softened until it faded into silence – like a wave building to a crest, crashing down, and whispering onto the sands.

After two or three waves of chanting had built and faded away, Clancy stopped politely clapping along. She leaned back on her elbows, stretched her legs out in front of her, and let her eyes nod closed. Cocooned by the music, she fell asleep.

30

Music and chanting wailed through Clancy's dreams, and she struggled awake to a terrible whining clamour, which she thought at first must be a smoke alarm. It wasn't until after she'd tumbled onto the floor in fright that she realised it was only a communal alarm clock blaring out in the corridor to wake people for yoga. She scrambled back into the bunk bed and buried her head in the pillow until someone turned it off.

Faint light filtered through the cracks between the curtains. Across the room, Clancy saw a single bed where Pa lay sleeping, his face creased into a frown. In the corner was another bed, with Bee curled tight under the covers. Above Clancy's head, Tash's legs wriggled over the edge of the top bunk, then her sister swung down to land with a soft thump on the carpet.

'Tash?' whispered Clancy. 'What time is it?'

'Sh!' Tash placed her lips ticklishly close to Clancy's ear and whispered, 'We're not allowed to talk till after breakfast.'

'O—' Clancy began to say *okay*, stopped herself, and gave Tash a thumbs-up instead, like Pa. Not allowed to talk? What kind of bizarre rule was that? How would anyone find out, anyway? Were the rooms bugged?

At least not talking wouldn't be a problem for Pa.

Bee gave a muffled groan, rolled over and shoved her head under her pillow. Clancy still didn't know what the time was. She waved to attract Tash's attention, and tapped her wrist where a watch would have been if she ever wore one.

Tash held up five fingers, then flashed both hands three times. *Five thirty.*

Clancy's jaw dropped in horror. With grimaces and gestures, she silently asked, *Are you getting up?*

Tash indicated herself, dressed and ready to go, and rolled her eyes. *Obviously!*

Clancy walked her fingers through the air and raised her eyebrows. *Where are you going?*

Tash pantomimed bending and stretching. Clancy shook her head, uncomprehending. At last Tash leaned close and hissed, *'Yoga!'*

Clancy could hear sounds of movement coming from the rest of the building – a running shower, shuffling footsteps, lights clicking on and off, doors opening and closing. But there were no voices. It was slightly creepy, like being surrounded by poltergeists.

Tash beckoned, and raised one eyebrow. (Clancy wished she'd inherited that gene.) *Coming?*

Clancy shook her head violently and snuggled back under the covers. *No way!*

Tash shrugged, waved goodbye, and slipped out of the room. Clancy lay still, listening to the soft noises outside, until the last door *whumped* shut and silence fell.

But not for long. Pa began fretfully snoring, and a riot of birdsong clamoured outside the window. Clancy sat up and squinted across at Bee, but her aunt was still curled in a tight ball, like a millipede, fast asleep – or at least pretending to be.

Quietly Clancy slid out of bed. She was still wearing her T-shirt and shorts, but she couldn't find her shoes. Were they still at reception? She tiptoed out into the corridor, and discovered several doors that opened to other guest rooms, and a bathroom, which she used. Wheelchair-friendly, she noted; without realising it, in the last couple of days she had begun to notice whether all kinds of things were wheelchair-friendly or not, from roads to doorways to toilets and showers.

She spotted her runners on a shelf by the front door of the building and pulled them on, easing the door closed behind her. Her heart bumped as she crept around the edges of a confusing warren of buildings, centred on the three-sided courtyard. But nobody seemed to be around; they must still be asleep or at early morning yoga with Tash...Clancy realised with a sudden pang that by falling asleep on the floor like a toddler – how embarrassing! – she'd missed out on stargazing with Toby.

The invisible birds were still shouting at the tops of their voices, and the grass was soaked with dew. Clancy tiptoed past a funny little mudbrick hut with no obvious purpose (a cubbyhouse? storage?), and a large pergola structure with a fire pit in the centre and plastic café walls like the dining room they'd sat in last night. Most of the buildings were made from weatherboards or mudbricks.

The rosy light of early morning spread across the sky, blotting out the stars. But the faithful pale moon was still there, swinging huge and low above the horizon. It was just a shade past full. This was definitely the real moon. The Magpie Bookshop's moon had been orbiting its own little world.

Clancy's racing heart slowed. It was peaceful here. She could see why Bee had decided to come, and why the magic of Nan had led them here.

Now she was beyond the buildings and onto the grass. A large stretch of cleared ground lay between her and the edge of the forest. Apart from the shrilling of the unseen birds, everything was still.

Clancy walked down a gentle slope to a dam, about the size of two swimming pools joined together. The damp grass brushed her ankles, and the rising sun touched the topmost leaves of the trees with gold. On the far side of the dam stood a large, imposing building of mudbrick and wood, some kind of hall or church or temple, with huge windows looking out onto the dam and the forest.

Clancy wandered closer, skirting the edge of the dam, cupped her hands to the glass, and peered inside.

The hall was filled with people. People standing on one leg, arms raised above their heads. People facing the window, hundreds of eyes staring straight at her.

Clancy sprang back, tripped and fell on her bum in the wet grass. Was Toby in there? Had he seen her? Not to mention Tash. She didn't dare to look. Her face burned as she hurried away, around the dam and across the grass until she reached the safety of the trees.

As she followed the walking track deeper into the forest, she still couldn't see any birds, but she could hear them shouting and twittering and calling and clamouring all around her. Sunlight slanted through the trees, lighting everything with gold, and wisps of mist drifted above the dry creek beds.

Far ahead of her on the winding path she glimpsed a figure, walking. It was a woman, wearing a wide-brimmed sun hat...One of the guests taking an early morning walk...or could it be...?

31

*N*an?

Clancy quickened her pace, but she couldn't seem to catch up; even when she broke into a run, the woman's figure was somehow always around the next bend.

At last she stopped, panting. If it wasn't Nan, she didn't want to catch up; if it was – well, Nan obviously didn't want to be caught. She rested for a moment, holding her side, and then she noticed something odd. She stepped off the path to take a closer look. It was the stump of a felled tree, with a pile of white stones sitting on top of it. Clancy stared, and walked all around it, but it made no sense.

'It's quartz. For healing.'

Clancy jumped. Bee had materialised beside her, robed in white as if she'd risen from the mists.

'We had a ceremony a few weeks ago.' Bee pointed to some other stumps, scattered through the forest, each with its own small heap of stones. 'It was to quiet the spirits.'

Maybe the spirits don't want to be quieted, thought Clancy. *Maybe they want to talk to us. Maybe they've got things to say...* But she didn't dare to say it aloud.

Clancy was growing used to the look of Bee's shaved head. In fact, with her white linen tunic and trousers and her elegant head like an Egyptian queen, she was starting to think Bee looked pretty amazing. Maybe not all changes were terrible after all.

Tentatively she whispered, 'Tash said we're not supposed to talk till after breakfast.'

'Oops,' said Bee; but she didn't seem to really care. Well, if Bee thought it was okay to break the rules, Clancy guessed it must be all right.

'There are so many birds in this forest,' she said. 'It's perfect for Pa.'

Bee looked uncomfortable. 'Clancy, sweetie, I need to talk to you about that...'

So it was going to be no, after all. Clancy wanted to protest: *but Nan brought us here!* But she couldn't quite say that to Bee, in spite of her talk about *the spirits*.

'Look, I get that poor Pa hates the place where he's living, and I get that you guys want to find him somewhere better. That's great, that's wonderful. You're amazing granddaughters. But – he can't stay here.'

Clancy kicked at the dead leaves on the forest floor. 'Why not? There are a ton of people here to help out. There's even a disabled bathroom.'

'I know, but that's for visitors. Someone like Pa can't live here full time. That's not what the ashram is for.'

'This place is an ashram?'

'Yes.'

'Okay.' Clancy took a breath. 'What's an ashram?'

'It's a community...We live together, we grow our own food, we learn about spirituality and meditation and Hinduism and vegetarianism and yoga...It's like a kind of school.'

'A yoga boarding school?'

'Sort of. Look, sweetie, I wouldn't have *time* to take care of Pa. I have classes, and I work in the kitchen and the garden...It's full-on.'

'How long are you going to stay here?'

'I don't know yet. Some people live here for years. I came four months ago, and I'm still here. I want to qualify as a yoga teacher.' Bee's face glowed. 'I love it here. It's amazing. I don't expect you to understand this, but it's brought parts of myself back together, when I was starting to feel like they were drifting apart – mind, body, spirit – I feel *whole* now.'

Clancy wasn't sure she understood exactly what Bee was talking about; but she grasped at the idea of everything pulling together, like the force of gravity. That felt right, that made sense. She thought of something else.

'What about your job in the city?'

'I quit. I hated that job. And I'm renting out my flat – that's how I'm paying for my retreat. Of course, Tash told me you met Alex...' Bee gave a sudden laugh. 'It's funny you and Tash turning up here with Pa, because when I think about it, the reason I'm here is actually because of Nan.'

Clancy jumped. 'What did you say?'

'Mum – your nan – used to practise yoga on the deck at Rosella. Do you remember that? Maybe you were too young. Pip and I used to do it with her sometimes – Pip not so much, she was too impatient. I always loved it, but after Mum died, I – let it go.' Bee's face took on a faraway look. 'Then one day I was wandering around in a secondhand bookshop, and I found this weird old hippie yoga instruction book, the same one that your nan always used. And I remembered how much I used to love doing yoga with her. So I bought the book, and I started practising, and joined some classes, and I got hooked. And here I am.'

Clancy's heart was beating fast. Cautiously she asked, 'Do you remember which bookshop it was?'

Bee screwed up her face. 'Not really – it was in the city. Near the library, I think? I can't remember the name. It was pretty run-down. It's probably closed by now.'

'Probably,' said Clancy sadly.

'Anyway...' Bee heaved a sigh. 'I don't think yoga is really Pa's thing.'

'Pretty hard to do yoga in a wheelchair. With one arm and one leg,' agreed Clancy.

'Definitely a challenge to sit in the lotus position. That means, with your legs crossed.'

'And he's not vegetarian, either...Bee, if this place is all about Indian stuff, how come there are no Indian people here?'

Bee looked startled. 'I don't know. Good question.'

There was a silence.

'So – what happens now?' said Clancy at last.

Bee shrugged. 'It's been lovely to see you all. An amazing surprise. But now you and Tash will have to take your grandpa back to the nursing home.'

'Have you told Tash that?' said Clancy.

'It's pretty obvious, isn't it?'

The sound of a distant gong reverberated across the grass. Bee put her arm around Clancy's shoulders. 'Come on. Time for breakfast.'

32

Clancy, Tash and Bee all found themselves in trouble with Jyotimitra when they arrived in the servery to collect their breakfast, because they'd left Pa on his own. Bee said she assumed Tash was in the bathroom when she'd decided to follow Clancy. 'I didn't know you were into yoga, sweetie. I didn't know you were into getting up at five-thirty.'

'I'm not, normally,' muttered Tash.

It was lucky Pa hadn't fallen, trying to climb out of bed, lucky that one of Toby's mothers, Jen, had popped in to see how they were managing, and found him there alone. (Unless it wasn't luck, of course, but Nan's magic.) Jen said afterwards that she didn't mind helping him into the wheelchair and taking him to the toilet. She'd even helped him have a shower, while Monica washed his clothes and hung them out to dry, and organised someone to fix the flat tyre on the wheelchair. But Clancy thought that she must have minded, a little. She was just too nice to say so.

Clancy and Tash found Pa sitting up at a table in the dining room in borrowed clothes, eating a bowl of muesli, with his hair wet and slicked down, his face scrubbed pink and shining.

Jen took Bee aside, and Clancy heard her murmur something. '...couldn't find his meds?'

But Bee shook her head and shrugged, and Jyotimitra, who seemed to be the boss of the ashram, beckoned her away.

After breakfast, they were allowed to talk again; but then it was time for something Bee called *karma yoga*, which meant everyone spending a couple of hours on ashram housework: cleaning bathrooms, vacuuming floors, emptying rubbish bins. Tash and Clancy didn't have to do it, but Bee and Toby and his mums did. And after karma yoga was finished, Bee reported, there would be a meeting with Jyotimitra, so they could figure out how to get Pa and Tash and Clancy back home.

'But we don't—'

'Don't start that again, Tash, please! We've talked about this already!' Bee held up one hand, and hurried away.

As everyone else dispersed for karma yoga, Tash and Clancy and Pa found themselves all alone in the dining room, with the plastic walls rolled up and the sun shining in and the smell of flowers in the air.

Clancy laid her hand on Pa's arm. 'You won't be able to stay here, Pa. Bee says they won't let you.'

'Sp-sp-sp.' Pa shrugged; he didn't seem surprised.

'They should,' said Tash. 'It's a commune, isn't it? Aren't communists supposed to be all about helping people? That's discrimination. It's ableist.'

'Toby's mums helped,' Clancy pointed out. 'They helped a *lot*.'

'But they're just visiting. They're going home today.' Tash rested her chin in her hands and frowned.

'The food's all vegetarian,' Clancy reminded her. 'Pa wouldn't like that, would you, Pa?'

'What?' said Pa irritably. 'Yeah, nah.'

Tash sat up straight. 'Forget Plan Bee. Time for Plan Pip.'

'But – where does Pip even live? How are you going to find out? If we ask Bee, she'll guess why we want to know.'

'I'm not going to *ask* her. I've got a better idea.' Tash glanced at Pa, but he wasn't listening. He seemed to have retreated into himself, brooding. He didn't even look up when a flock of rainbow lorikeets swooped overhead, squawking cheerfully.

Tash said, 'I'm going to need your help. Both of you.'

They didn't realise it until afterwards, but it was the perfect time to stage a raid on the office, because everyone else at the ashram was busy performing karma yoga. The kitchen was full of people chopping vegetables for lunch, vacuum cleaners hummed, and in the distance people trudged back and forth from the sheds with rubbish bins. But the reception area and the office were deserted.

Cautiously Clancy wheeled Pa into the foyer. 'You're the lookout,' Tash told him. 'If you see anyone coming, make a noise. And don't let them into the office – stall them.'

Pa brightened, and the twinkle came back into his eyes. Clancy was beginning to realise that Pa, like Tash, enjoyed making mischief. Clancy wondered wistfully if Nan had been like that, too. In her photographs, she looked pretty twinkly-eyed. Maybe this whole long adventure was Nan's idea of a fun weekend?

Hey, Nan? Clancy sent out a silent message as Tash tried the office door. *If you're here, could you give us a hand? Please?*

The handle turned and the door swung open. *Thanks, Nan!* thought Clancy, as she and Tash crept inside. Her heart thumped. Breaking and entering – twice. This wasn't going to look good when the police finally caught up with them. Unless Nan could take care of that, too.

Tash closed the door and flipped the lock. Clancy shot her an anxious glance, scared they'd be trapped in there.

Tash misread her sister's expression. 'Don't look at me like that!' she hissed. 'We're not trying to steal anything. We just want to look at Bee's file. If this place really is like a school or a camp or whatever, then I bet there were a million forms to fill out.'

'So?' whispered Clancy.

'Think about it – next of kin, emergency contacts. Who do they call if she goes into anaphylactic shock?

I bet it's Pip.' Tash pointed to the desk. 'You look on the computer, I'll check the filing cabinet.'

Clancy crept across to the computer and knelt on the floor behind the desk, so she could duck underneath if anyone came in.

The ashram might have been run by hippies, but they still had *some* security. Clancy whispered over to Tash, who was already rifling through the drawers of the filing cabinet, 'Password protected!'

'Bugger!' muttered Tash, just like Pa; then, inspired, she whispered, 'Try *hari om*.'

'What?'

'Everyone says it here. You must have heard them? They chanted it after kirtan last night and before yoga this morning. And it's written everywhere, on the bottom of every notice. I guess it means God bless you, or amen, or something.' Tash spelled it out aloud, and sure enough, that was the password. Clancy was impressed. Usually her sister didn't notice details like that.

Clancy wasn't a computer geek, but she knew enough to find her way around a basic filing system, and the ashram's filing system was very basic. It didn't take her long to find the spreadsheet with the names of all the weekend visitors and retreat participants (which she guessed would include Toby and his mothers, though she didn't waste time looking them up), and the database of permanent residents, and at last the file they needed: a list of students. That sounded like Bee.

Clancy clicked on the file and searched for Beatrice Sanderson. And up came all her details: date of birth, birth name, spiritual name (Atma), medical history (in case you popped a blood vessel standing on your head, Clancy guessed), how long she'd been studying yoga (all her life, according to Bee, which seemed like a slight exaggeration to Clancy), and, just as Tash had predicted, an emergency contact. And Tash was right: Philippa Sanderson was listed as Bee's next of kin.

Relationship: twin.

'Hurry up!' hissed Tash.

'I'll print it out,' whispered Clancy. But she'd just clicked on the print icon when they heard a terrible moaning and groaning coming from the reception area. Actually it was lucky that Pa was making so much noise, because it helped to disguise the whirr of the printer coming to life.

'Where is it?' Frantically Tash looked round. Clancy couldn't see the printer either, but the noise seemed to be coming from the corner of the room. She pointed in what she guessed was the right direction and left Tash to hunt down the printer while she closed the files and tried to leave the computer as she'd found it.

Meanwhile, Pa was making the most alarming noises in the foyer. Clancy risked a peep through the glass window in the office door and saw him surrounded by a group of murmuring middle-aged women in activewear, wearing concerned expressions, all saying things like *does your chest hurt?* and *is anyone with you?* Pa clutched his heart and groaned even louder. He caught Clancy's eye and gave her the most enormous wink. Clancy ducked back below the window and then she saw it – the printer, on the floor, half-hidden by a pile of folders with mandala symbols on them. *Thanks, Nan!*

'Tash!' Clancy whispered. 'I found it!' She crawled over and ripped out the sheet of paper with Pip's address. Then she heard a loud female voice saying, 'Where's that woman who says she's a nurse?'

Another voice cried, 'I'll call an ambulance!' and the handle of the office door rattled.

Clancy froze. They were trapped!

Tash beckoned wildly, and Clancy commando-crawled across the carpet to where her sister was holding open a second door at the rear of the office.

'Sp-sp-sp!' cried Pa, probably trying to tell the worried women that he was *fine now, thanks, no ambulance necessary!*

Clancy and Tash found themselves in a small store-room, lined with shelves of stationery, which led in turn to another room, a larger office space with a couple of desks and a window. Tash shoved the window open and somersaulted out onto the grass. Clancy had to drag a chair to the window and clamber up, but Tash yanked her over the windowsill and Clancy fell on top of her.

33

They lay for a few seconds, winded, in a sheltered garden hedged with thick bushes. Tash, of course, recovered first. 'Come on!' She bounced up and dragged Clancy around the corner of the building.

'Here, take it, take it!' Clancy thrust the paper at her sister and Tash crammed it into her pocket. Clancy hastily patted her own pocket, but Nan was still in there.

They emerged into the main courtyard, where people were strolling around with mugs of tea. Apparently karma yoga was over. Clancy and Tash hurried to the reception area to rescue Pa from his rescuers.

'Pa! Are you okay?' cried Clancy. She was a terrible liar, but she wasn't a bad actor. She threw herself at Pa and he gave her a one-armed hug as the knot of concerned women scattered out of the way.

Tash marched up to them. 'He probably needs a glass of water. And fresh air. Don't crowd him. He feels faint if he's too hot.'

Obediently, still murmuring, the women drew back so Tash could wheel Pa outside. Someone brought water and they parked in the shade while Pa fanned himself with one hand. He really didn't look very well; he was an even better actor than Clancy. He gave her another wink at one point, and Clancy was scared that someone would notice and think he was having another stroke, but luckily nobody did. One by one the ladies drifted away, saying things like *he seems all right now* and *I'll tell Lesley not to worry about finding the nurse*.

When they'd all gone, Tash wheeled Pa out of the courtyard, down toward the big hall, to a secluded spot under a tree where there was a bench looking out over the dam. Pa's glass of water sloshed onto his borrowed pants.

'Sp-sp!' said Pa crossly, plucking at the wet cloth.

'Aren't you going to ask if we got it?' said Tash.

'Sp-sp?'

'Well, we did. Thanks to Clancy.'

'Sp-sp!' Pa gave Clancy a high-five as Tash spread the paper out onto her knee.

Pip's address was in Cockatoo Bay.

'Where's that?' said Clancy.

Tash rolled her eyes. 'On the coast.'

'Well, duh,' said Clancy.

'On the Great Ocean Road,' Tash clarified. 'Miranda's grandparents' holiday house is round there somewhere.

We drove through Cockatoo Bay that Easter when I stayed with her.'

Geography was not Clancy's strong point, though she was pretty good at European countries because she was a fan of the Eurovision Song Contest. Feeling very businesslike, she said, 'Train? Or taxi?'

Tash gave her a look. 'A taxi would cost about three hundred dollars. Maybe more. And there's no train. Only buses. I know we've still got Pa's stash, but that is way too much money to waste on a taxi.'

Clancy's heart sank. She couldn't see how even Nan's moony superpowers were going to solve this one. 'So how are we going to get there?'

'Let me think.' Tash threw herself back on the grass and covered her eyes with her arm, which is why she didn't see Toby coming.

'Hey,' he said, and Tash jumped.

Clancy laughed, Pa smiled, and Toby grinned as he lowered himself to the grass beside Clancy. 'Just me. Nothing to be scared of.'

'She was thinking,' said Clancy.

'Yeah? Thinking about what?'

'Logistics,' said Tash crossly.

'Anything I can help with?'

Tash pointed. 'Me, him, her. To Cockatoo Bay. Today. Preferably before Bee – I mean Atma – organises to stick us on a train back to the city. Any ideas welcome.'

Toby stretched out his long legs. The sunlight glinted on his black curls. 'Why Cockatoo Bay?'

'Your job is to come up with answers,' said Tash. 'Not more questions.'

'Our aunt lives there,' Clancy told him. 'Another one of Pa's daughters. It's Plan C. This was Plan B, but it hasn't worked out. So Pip is Plan C. Because she's by the sea—' Clancy heard herself babbling, and shut up.

When Toby smiled, two small dimples appeared by the corners of his mouth. 'You guys all fitted into our car okay last night, didn't you?'

'Eventually. After the wheelchair folded up.'

'We-ell,' said Toby. 'It just so happens that I was going to ask my mums to drop me at Cockatoo Bay anyway. And I reckon if we were giving you guys a lift, they might just do it.'

'Seriously?' gasped Clancy. Nan's magic was at work again!

Tash sat up, squinting at Toby suspiciously. 'Why do you want to go to Cockatoo Bay?'

'I thought you were looking for answers?' said Toby. 'Not more questions?'

'Ha ha,' said Tash. 'Seriously, why?'

Toby scratched his nose. 'A mate from school's staying down there for summer. He invited me down after Christmas, but I'd already promised Mum and Ma I'd come here.' His pale face turned slightly pink. 'We used to come here every year when I was a kid. Mum and Ma love it, and they guilted me into it...'

'I think it's kind of cool here, to be honest,' said Clancy.

Toby shot her a surprised, grateful glance, and the colour in his cheeks faded. He scrambled up. 'I'll ask my mums. Give me an hour to work on them. I reckon they'll say yes. They love helping people out. A nurse and a social worker, what do you expect?'

Toby waved cheerfully as he walked back up the grassy slope to the ashram buildings.

'Sp-sp-sp!' said Pa.

'Yeah, he's okay, I guess,' admitted Tash grudgingly.

He's lovely, Clancy wanted to say; but she knew how Tash would react if she did. And she didn't like Toby like *that*; she just thought he was a good person. Everyone was going to start getting all romantic next year, she supposed crossly, now they were starting high school... *This* year. Bugger.

'Sp-sp-sp?' Pa was asking Tash.

Tash said, 'He's not my type.'

Relief was Clancy's first reaction. Then she said, 'Who is your type, Tash?' It had never occurred to Clancy to ask this before. It struck her that, in spite of sharing a house and some DNA with her, there were a lot of things she didn't know about her sister.

'None of your business,' said Tash instantly. 'But not him. You can have him, peanut.'

And there it was. 'I don't want him,' said Clancy crossly. 'I don't want anybody.'

'Oh, relax,' said Tash kindly. 'Everyone dates *someone* one day. Even you.'

Clancy was silent. But maybe Tash was right. Logically, just as Pa and Antonia and Nan had once been young, it was fairly likely (unless there was a tragic accident) that she, Clancy, would be old one day... Old enough to date, anyway.

Pa shifted uncomfortably in his chair, and sighed. 'Sp-sp-sp...'

Clancy reached for his hand, and they sat and watched the birds.

34

At eleven o'clock (which felt much later, after their early start), a gong sounded. Everybody dropped whatever they were doing – preparing lunch, gardening, meditating, taking yoga classes – and headed for the big church-like hall by the dam. Bee caught up with Clancy and Tash and Pa and beckoned for them to go in, too.

'Yoga nidra is for everyone,' she said, eyeing Clancy. 'Including you.' She ran her hand over the dark stubble of her head. 'Jyotimitra's arranged a lift for you, back to the station at Quoll Creek, in time for the two o'clock train. Just to keep everybody off your back, I told her I'd called your dad, and he's meeting you at the other end.'

'*Is* he?' Clancy's heart leapt.

Tash gave her a withering look. 'Of course he isn't. How could he get back from New Zealand so fast?' She said gruffly, 'Thanks for that, Bee…I mean, Atma. And don't worry about that ride to the station. Toby's mums have already offered to drop us off.'

'Oh. Okay.' Bee lowered her voice. 'You realise I've lied for you? I don't feel good about that. It's bad karma. But...' She chewed her lip. 'I don't want anyone to know I'm here. Not yet, anyway. I don't want any lectures from the family about quitting my job and blah blah blah. So how about you keep my secret, and I'll keep yours.'

'Deal,' said Tash instantly.

Bee said, 'So you promise you'll take Pa straight back to the nursing home?'

'You can trust us,' said Tash evasively.

'And you'll be all right on the train?'

'We'll be fine.'

'You'd better give me a call when you're back at Polly's and let me know you've arrived safely. Leave a message for me at the front desk.'

'Okay.'

'Good.' Bee sighed, obviously relieved that they wouldn't be her problem anymore. 'Come and do yoga nidra. Everyone loves yoga nidra. It's the highlight of the day.'

Clancy shook her head. 'I can't do yoga. I don't bend.'

Bee laughed. 'You don't need to bend. Even Pa can do yoga nidra.'

Inside the big hall, the ceiling soared and the hall was filled with cool, hushed light. There was no furniture, just an empty carpeted floor and a low platform at the far end. If Clancy had been a little kid, she might have been tempted to spread her arms and zoom around the almost empty space. But because she was technically a high school student now (*help*!), she copied the adults, and took a yoga mat and a blanket from the neat stacks by the wall. Jyotimitra was sitting cross-legged on the platform in her orange robes, eyes closed, like a teacher waiting for her class to settle down.

Bee rolled Pa to a corner at the back of the hall and touched her finger to her lips. *Huh*, thought Clancy. As if Pa would have a problem keeping quiet.

Clancy stayed near the back too, so she could copy what other people did and not make a fool of herself. Silently each person found a spot, unfurled their mat and lay down. It reminded Clancy of nap time at kinder. Toby gave her a grin and a thumbs-up as he walked past, and Clancy relaxed; if she did mess something up, at least he wouldn't be able to see her.

Not that she cared what Toby thought.

Clancy lay on her back with the rug spread over her, arms by her sides, like everyone else, and gazed up at the ceiling. Fans spun slow and silent overhead. Gradually all the little rustles and creaks and sighs died away, and quiet settled over the hall like snow. Clancy wasn't sure if she was supposed to close her eyes or not.

Jyotimitra began to speak.

Her voice was deep and slow, like thick dark honey, like golden syrup, like gravity. Clancy could feel her heartbeat calming as she listened. She had a sudden flash of memory from when she was very small, of lying in bed at the house at Rosella, listening to a relaxation tape, while baby Bruno cried in the next room. And she knew that it had been Nan who'd played that tape for her and Tash, to help them fall asleep.

But Jyotimitra was better than the tape. Though there were nearly a hundred people in the hall, Clancy felt that Jyotimitra was speaking just to her. She forgot that she was far from home, forgot that they'd failed to find a new place for Pa to live, forgot the looming terrors of high school, forgot that there wasn't one thing she was better at than Tash, forgot that her family was scattered over hundreds of miles, forgot her fears and her doubts, forgot that the universe was slowly but surely flying apart. All of that melted away, dissolved in the deep molten flow of Jyotimitra's words.

Bringing your attention to the right thumb...the fingers of the right hand...the palm of the right hand... the back of the hand. The forearm...the elbow.

A heavy, delicious warmth travelled around the whole of Clancy's body. Her eyes closed, her jaw relaxed.

Now the voice asked her to focus on the sounds nearby: her own breathing, a muffled sneeze, an insect bumbling against the window glass. Then on the sounds that were further away: a breeze brushing the leaves, a distant bird. *Hear the sounds, and let them go.* Each small sound wove into the tapestry of the huge, peaceful silence, and merged with it; a tiny star of sound in a vast universe of darkness.

Clancy floated in the velvet dark. She was safe, and warm, like firelight, like a quilt wrapped around her shoulders, like snuggling into her grandmother's lap, like sinking into her own bed back home, like soft feathers, like sleep...

Look up, Clancy. Look up at the sky.

It was Nan's comfortable voice, and she could feel the warmth of Nan's body beside her, standing out on the deck at Rosella in the dark, and she could smell Nan's lily-of-the-valley perfume. The memory was so suddenly vivid, it burst over her like a firework.

Like a small steady flame, like a silver moon, like a book fallen open to the right page, like birdsong in her mind, Nan was there.

See the stars, Clancy? See the moon?

Clancy floated, held in Nan's arms, safe and warm and loved, gazing at the sky. And every star shone in its rightful place, the planets looped in their steady orbits, the friendly moon smiled down.

Everything where it belongs...

And then, too soon, much too soon, Jyotimitra's voice thrust itself rudely into a crack in Clancy's mind.

'Bringing your awareness back to the room. In your own time, allowing your toes and fingers to gently move. In your own time, allowing your eyes to open...'

Don't go, Nan! Clancy pleaded silently. *Nan! Are we doing the right thing? Is everything going to be okay? Tell me!*

But against her will, her eyes were blinking open. The high, soaring roof of the hall and the spinning fans swam back into focus. Desperately she screwed her eyes shut again, trying to plunge herself back into the welcoming dark.

But Nan was gone.

All around, Clancy heard small sighs and rustlings as people shifted and coughed. Someone in the middle of the room was snoring peacefully, fast asleep.

Jyotimitra said, 'Please remember to keep *mouna*, silence, until lunch is over.'

Slowly Clancy sat up. Her experience had been so real, so vivid, she almost expected to see Nan stretching beside her on the next mat. She took in a big sniff, but no waft of lily-of-the-valley met her nostrils. She pressed her face into her knees to hide hot tears of disappointment.

All around the hall, people drew themselves into the lotus position, legs crossed, facing Jyotimitra. In unison, everyone chanted, '*Om – om – om – hari om*.'

Jyotimitra bowed. '*Hari om tat sat*.'

'*Hari om tat sat*,' they all murmured.

There was a moment's silence and stillness, then all over the hall there was a stirring as people stood up and stretched and gathered their possessions. Clancy rolled up her mat, folded her blanket, and placed them by the wall. A pulse of anger and bitterness beat in her temple. Not fair, not fair! For Nan to come so close, then disappear, without telling her if it was all going to work out – that was cheating!

But everyone else seemed to be moving around in a dream of bliss. At the back of the hall, she saw Bee, with a serene expression, take the handles of Pa's wheelchair. Tash was drifting like a sleepwalker, as slowly as Clancy had ever seen her quicksilver sister move. There was Toby, with a solemn, glowing expression, and his two mums with their fingers intertwined, exchanging a private smile.

Only Pa still seemed unmoved, pulling crossly at his trousers. Would Bee realise that meant he wanted the toilet? Clancy hoped they'd make it in time.

As she marched out into the too-bright sunshine, a cluster of lorikeets rose as one and scattered overhead, their jewel-bright colours gleaming. But Clancy dropped her head. The sky held no answers for her. She couldn't believe that Nan had let her down.

35

A couple of hours later, they were on the road to Cockatoo Bay, crammed into Jen and Monica's car. Pa sat in the front seat next to Monica, with Jen and Tash behind them, hemmed in with bags and bedding. Toby had wanted to drive, but with so many passengers on board, his mothers wouldn't let him. So he'd taken down the L-plates from the front and back windows, and squeezed himself next to Clancy in the cramped seats at the rear. The folded wheelchair just fitted in the narrow luggage space behind them.

Clancy heard Monica trying to talk to Pa, but it was hard work when she couldn't turn to see his face or his one-handed gestures. Pa responded to her friendly questions and comments on the view with a grunt or a shrug, and after a while Monica lapsed into silence, and Pa's head nodded as he drifted into sleep.

The road wound deep into the forest, dropping down into steep valleys and climbing up hills, twisting and turning through tree-ferns and tall timber.

Clancy felt guilty that they hadn't told Bee the truth. Bee had done her best; she deserved better than that. Even though she suspected that Bee wouldn't have approved of Plan C...Clancy imagined her aunt seeing them now, not obediently climbing on the train back to the city, but heading for the sea. Would Bee be confused, or worried, or angry?

Clancy contemplated the back of her sister's head as Tash chatted to Jen about football. She didn't seem to have thought about Bee at all. Life must be so easy for Tash; she never worried about other people's feelings. Did she tell herself it was okay to upset people, or let them tell lies for her, if it was for a higher purpose, like Bee said? Or did she not think about it at all? Was that a better way to live? Tash made things happen; she got things done. But if she trampled over people on the way, was it worth it? *If it had been left to me,* Clancy reminded herself, *Pa would still be stuck at The Elms...*

Suddenly Clancy understood a saying that had never made sense to her before, something about the ends justifying the means. That was Tash's way, to concentrate on the end results and never mind anything else. But Clancy worried so much about the means that she never made it all the way to the ends. She never even made it as far as the beginnings, half the time! Maybe you needed both kinds of people in the world, the Tashes to kidnap Pa from The Elms, and the Clancys to watch out for the signals from Nan that kept them on the right path.

With a shock, it occurred to Clancy that perhaps she and her sister made a good team.

All this time, Toby had been listening to something through his earbuds. Now he let out a sudden snort of laughter that made Clancy jump.

'Sorry.' He yanked out one wire. 'It's *The Grandfather Paradox*.'

'Is that a band?'

'No, it's a podcast. You don't know it? Well, the grandfather paradox is a science fiction trope, time travel, you know? Like, if you travel back in time and kill your own grandfather, how could you be born in the first place to go back and kill him?'

'I know what the grandfather paradox is,' said Clancy.

'Yeah? Are you into spec fic?'

Clancy struggled with her answer before admitting, 'Not really.' But what if she told him, *I think I might have actually time travelled, though? Maybe?*

He would think she was insane, that's what.

Toby waved a hand. 'Never mind. This has nothing to do with spec fic anyway. It's a science podcast about space travel, astronomy, quantum mechanics...pretty nerdy stuff,' he added hastily, his cheeks flushing pink. 'But funny.'

'Could I—?'

'Sure!' He passed her an earbud and they both leaned in toward his phone to listen. Clancy didn't understand the whole thing, but it was interesting, and she got at least some of the jokes.

When it was finished, Clancy removed the earbud and said impulsively, 'Do you ever worry about entropy?'

'Worry about it? No, not really. I mean, it's just kind of *there*. You can't do much about it, can you? It's a universal law.'

'I think that's what worries me,' said Clancy. 'That eventually everything is just going to fall into ruins, drift apart, disintegrate, and there's nothing we can do to stop it.'

Toby considered this for a moment. 'What about gravity?'

'What about it?'

'When planets are forming, and all the random pieces of rock and asteroid and dust and gas are floating around in space, gravity pulls them together, right? They clump together, and that's how you get planets and moons. Gravity brings them together.'

'So...gravity is the opposite of entropy?'

'Probably not. I reckon it's more complicated than that. But still.'

'Still,' agreed Clancy, feeling encouraged. 'Hey, Toby? I was wondering something. If the universe is infinite, and there are infinite stars, how come the sky at night isn't totally lit up with starlight? Shouldn't there be stars shining in every bit of space there is?'

'Ah, Olber's paradox,' said Toby at once. 'But the universe isn't infinite. There aren't infinite stars. That's why the sky isn't lit up all the time. Hang on, the guys talked about that on the podcast once. I'll see if I can find it.'

Clancy found it oddly reassuring to think that there were limits to the universe. She and Toby were talking so intently about space, about podcasts and about videos, that it seemed like no time before Tash sang out, 'I can see the sea!'

For most of the year, the coastal towns were sleepy hamlets, almost deserted. But in summer, they exploded with tourists. The traffic was so thick, their car was forced to crawl along at walking speed. Tash fidgeted in her seat. If it hadn't been for Pa, she would have jumped out. Pa woke up and stared blearily through the window.

'Well, this is a shocker!' said Monica cheerfully.

Caravans lined the narrow strip of land between the road and the beach; people draped in towels sauntered along the pavement. The shops overflowed and cars crowded the parking spaces.

Toby gave Clancy a nudge. 'The power of attraction. All these people, coming to the beach.' He banged his fists together. 'Like a magnet. Like gravity.'

As someone who wasn't fond of crowds, Clancy couldn't help thinking that this particular force was a little too powerful for her liking. The town was bigger than she'd expected, a bewildering jumble of shabby beach shacks and brand new townhouses with stone feature walls and huge windows facing the ocean. The car inched along the streets.

'Which way to your aunt's place, Tash?'

Pa gave a sudden cry, and his hand shot out.

'Here?' Monica slammed on the brakes and they were all thrown forward. Behind them, a horn blared, and someone yelled angrily.

Pa twisted his head to speak to Tash and Clancy. 'Sp-sp!'

'Just a bird,' explained Clancy. 'Sorry.'

'Oh.' Monica took a breath, and the car rolled forward again.

'Here,' said Tash abruptly. 'You can let us out here.'

'Is this it?'

'Near enough. We can walk from here.' Tash fumbled with her seatbelt.

'We'll drive you in—'

'No driveway!' said Tash. 'This is fine. Seriously.'

Monica pulled over and they all piled out. Jen and Toby helped Pa, groaning and complaining, to shuffle himself clumsily out of the front seat and drop heavily into the wheelchair, which Monica and Tash had unfolded.

'Like a well-oiled machine!' said Jen, beaming.

Clancy dug Tash's pack from the back seat.

'That's it?' said Monica. 'Wow, you guys travel light.'

Tash fished out her wallet. 'Here's some petrol money.'

Monica's eyes flashed. 'Put that away! We don't want your money.'

'It's karma.' Jen lunged for Tash, arms wide for a hug. 'You can do us a favour one day. Send us tickets to your first professional football game.'

'Deal.' Tash accepted the hug. 'Thanks. You guys are the best. Seriously.'

'Tobes?' said Monica. 'You want to drive to Liam's? Or are we dropping you here, too?'

Clancy looked at the road. She could feel Toby's eyes on her, but she didn't dare to look at him. Her face glowed warm. She couldn't speak. The pause grew longer.

Then she heard Nan's voice, just as she'd heard it during yoga nidra that morning. *Look up, Clancy. Look up!*

Before she could give herself a chance to think about it, Clancy looked up and her eyes met Toby's. She found herself smiling at him, and his face dropped into a grin of relief.

'I'll get out here, too, I reckon,' he said. 'I can help these guys with the wheelchair.'

'All right, love.' Monica gave him a hug.

Jen hugged him next, and he dragged his sports bag from the car. At the last minute, he took his L-plates, too.

'Hey!' Jen waved a finger. 'No driving with Liam. No driving without a licensed person, okay?'

'I'm not an idiot.' Toby looked offended. 'But just in case I get the chance – gotta get my hours up.'

'Well, be careful.' Jen gave him a final hug and climbed into the front seat.

'Sp-sp-sp!' Pa raised his hand in farewell.

The doors slammed, the engine roared, and Jen and Monica were gone.

36

The four of them stood on the pavement in the afternoon sun.

Clancy ventured, 'Which one is Pip's house, Tash?'

Tash frowned down the street after the vanished car, pulled out her ponytail and retied it.

Toby looked from Clancy to Tash and back again. 'You do know where it is, right?'

Tash didn't answer. Clancy faltered, 'Not exactly...'

Toby said, 'I can look it up on my phone, if you want?'

Tash's frown deepened. It was clear she'd rather gnaw off her own hand than admit she needed help.

Clancy took a breath. 'Thanks, Toby. That would be great.'

Crossly Tash seized the handles of Pa's wheelchair. 'It's Garner Street,' she said shortly.

'Got it,' said Toby after a moment. 'It's a bit of a walk.'

'Why didn't you look it up before, Tash?' said Clancy.

'Use your peabrain, Clarice,' snapped Tash. 'A: looked

it up how? And B: if they'd taken us straight there, they would have seen Pip being all, *what are you doing here?*'

'Hang on,' said Toby. 'Your aunt doesn't know you're coming?'

'Cockatoo Bay isn't that big,' said Tash briskly, beginning to march Pa along the pavement. 'It won't take long.'

'It looks big enough to me,' muttered Clancy.

Toby gave her a conspiratorial grin.

Pa put up his hand to shield his eyes from the sun's glare. 'Sp-sp-sp!'

'I agree,' said Clancy. 'We should have brought hats.'

'Give me a freaking break,' said Tash. 'I can't think of everything.'

They traipsed along the streets for what felt like hours, but was only about forty-five minutes, from one end of Cockatoo Bay to the other. Sweat trickled down Clancy's back and her eyes stung. She thought she might pass out, right there on the footpath. Only the shame of fainting in front of Toby kept her upright. Pa slumped in his chair, hiding his face behind his hand. The sun seemed brighter by the sea, as if it were glittering off salt crystals suspended in the air.

'I can push for a bit,' offered Toby.

Clancy thought that Tash would refuse, but silently her sister stepped back and allowed Toby to take the handles.

'Wow,' said Toby after a few moments. 'I can really feel my arm muscles.'

'Yep,' said Tash grimly.

Toby was still gamely pushing when Clancy, who was supposed to be navigating, squinted at the next signpost and gave a yelp. 'Garner Street!'

'Number ten,' said Tash. 'There it is.'

They halted outside a dilapidated fibro house, one of the old beach shacks, painted a faded blue, with a sagging verandah. The house stood like a lonely island in a sea of yellowed grass, with a single lemon tree drooping to one side. A battered old car slumped in the cracked driveway.

'Well,' said Tash. 'Here goes nothing.'

She ran up the steps to the front door. *Steps*, noted Clancy automatically. *That's not good.* Now they were finally here, what was Pip going to say?

'Sp-sp,' groaned Pa, waving toward the shade of the lemon tree, and Toby heaved the chair across the grass. Clancy huddled behind Pa as Tash rapped at the screen door, then jumped back as the door smacked open and Pip stepped outside.

'Oh. My. God,' said Pip. 'You're actually here.'

Clancy barely recognised her aunt. Pip's thick hair was dragged back in a bushy ponytail, and her belly ballooned out in front of her, her T-shirt rising up over the taut globe of skin. Half-drum, half-human, a built-in one-woman band.

'Oh, fabulous,' said Tash in disgust. 'You're *pregnant*.'

'Sp-sp-sp?' asked Pa in fretful bewilderment.

'Pip's having a baby,' Clancy told him. 'You're going to be a grandfather again! We're going to have a baby cousin!'

'Hah!' said Pa.

Pip pushed past Tash and waddled down the steps to give him a hug.

'Sp-sp-sp!'

'Sorry, Dad.' Pip looked at Clancy. 'I don't get it.'

'He says congratulations. He's really happy for you.'

Though in fact, Pa looked more stunned than happy. 'Sp-sp-sp?'

'Why didn't you tell us?' translated Clancy.

Pip's face screwed up. 'Long story...not important now.' Her voice hardened and Clancy's gut twisted like a wrung rag. 'Do you guys have *any* idea how much trouble you're in? What the hell are you doing here? And who's this?' She glared at Toby. 'When Polly rang, I told her she was crazy to think you might come, but no, here you are. Where the hell have you *been*? Do you realise there's a manhunt for you? Did you know Tim and Harriet are flying back from New Zealand to look for you? The *police* are looking for you. Polly's out of her *mind!*'

Clancy shrank back behind the wheelchair as Pip went on and on.

'Do you want me to go?' whispered Toby.

Without realising it, Clancy grabbed his arm. 'Not yet...'

'Sp-sp-sp?' murmured Pa, confused.

'She's not very happy with us,' Clancy whispered back, a lump in her throat.

'Oh, bugger,' whispered Pa.

Tash folded her arms. 'We came here to ask for your help.'

'Oh, really?' Pip hauled herself back onto the verandah so she could yell at Tash at closer range. 'I have a couple of issues of my own to deal with right now, if you haven't noticed...'

Clancy stared miserably at the grass as the argument raged on, Pip and Tash shouting over the top of each other.

Nothing to do with me – it's not fair – you're part of this family, too – who asked you anyway?

Toby shifted uncomfortably from foot to foot, and Clancy was terrified that he might take off at any minute. She felt sick. She hated to hear people fighting, even random strangers on the bus or kids at school. Also, she was desperately thirsty, but she didn't dare push past Tash and Pip to go inside for a glass of water.

Why had Nan brought them here? This can't have been what she wanted. Why was everything falling apart?

Clancy became aware that Pa was moaning softly, and suddenly she couldn't bear it anymore. 'Shut up!' she screamed. 'Stop it! Stop it *now*!'

Shocked into silence, Pip and Tash turned to stare at her.

Just then Pa let out a loud groan, his eyes squeezed shut, sweat beading on his forehead.

'You see?' cried Clancy. 'You're upsetting Pa!'

Pa groaned again. His left hand fluttered out and clutched at his side.

'I think it's more than that,' said Toby quietly. 'I think there's something wrong.'

37

As soon as Toby said it, Clancy knew he was right. Pa had been miserable ever since they'd left Quoll Creek – no, she realised with a shock, ever since they'd left the city. His face looked grey beneath the stubble.

'He's fine! He's just tired,' said Tash. 'Aren't you, Pa?'

Clancy knelt beside the wheelchair. 'Pa? Are you okay?'

Pa shook his head. He lifted his hand and mimed putting something into his mouth.

'Thirsty?' guessed Tash. Without waiting to ask Pip's permission, she dashed into the house, hurried out a moment later with a glass of water and bounded down the steps.

Pa sipped, then groaned, 'Nah, nah,' and pushed the glass back into Tash's hand.

'Are you hungry, Godfrey?' asked Toby.

'Hang on, Dad.' Pip waddled inside, then came out carrying a muesli bar, a banana, a packet of chocolate biscuits and a potato. But Pa turned away in revulsion from it all.

'Pa? Have you got a pain?' asked Clancy.

His eyes squeezed shut, Pa nodded tightly.

'Headache? Stomachache? I've got Panadol,' said Pip. 'Somewhere.'

'No, no,' groaned Pa, and again he made that gesture of putting something into his mouth.

Clancy gasped. 'His pills! Pa's medication! Have you been taking your pills, Pa?'

Pa shook his head, and threw up his hand. *Finally*.

'Where are they?' Tash snapped her fingers and Clancy shrugged off the backpack and tipped everything out onto the grass. The books, Tash's wallet, her hoodie, the tin containing the remains of the stash of cash, train tickets, hair ties, a comb, deodorant, toothbrush, tampons, an empty water bottle, all cascaded at their feet. But no pills.

Tash swore. 'I think we left them at Rosella.'

'I didn't pick them up,' said Clancy.

'Me either.'

They stared at each other, stricken.

Pip said, 'I'm going to call an ambulance.'

'No!' cried Pa.

'Hospital's the best place, Dad. They can look after you there. You know I'm right.'

'No!' Pa reached up to clutch Clancy's hand. Tears were in his eyes. 'No no no no no…'

'He hates hospitals,' said Tash. 'You can't force him to go if he doesn't want to.'

'It doesn't matter if he hates them or not,' said Pip. 'If he needs to go, he needs to go.'

Clancy sensed that the shouting was about to start up again. She gazed imploringly at Toby, though she didn't really think he'd be able to help.

But he did. He touched Pa's sleeve and asked gently, 'Godfrey? If you don't want to go to hospital, what do you want to do?'

Pa opened his eyes. He freed his hand from Clancy's and pointed, far into the distance, in the direction of the city.

'Go back to The Elms?' said Clancy.

'No!' shouted Pa, and pointed more emphatically.

'To Rosella?' said Tash.

'Yes!'

Tash and Clancy looked at each other.

Pip folded her arms above her belly. 'I still say he'd be better off in hospital.'

'No point,' said Tash triumphantly. 'Because we don't know what medication Pa's on, and he can't tell them.'

It wasn't until later that Clancy realised that they could have called The Elms, and she wondered why none of them had thought of that.

'Could he write it down?' said Toby.

Pip shook her head. 'He can't write anymore, or spell. All his letters are gone.'

'He can still read though,' put in Tash. 'Which is so weird.'

Clancy said, 'At least at Rosella, his pills are all there, packaged up, ready to go.'

Tash looked at Toby. 'Lend me your phone, and I'll call a taxi. Assuming they have maxi-taxis out here.'

'Hey!' said Pip. 'Cockatoo Bay isn't the outback, you know. We have taxis.'

Sunday night. Streets clogged with traffic. A taxi might not arrive for hours, thought Clancy in despair.

She looked around from where she knelt beside Pa's chair. Everyone seemed paralysed, as if someone had pressed pause: Toby holding his phone, Tash's hand out demanding it, Pip with feet planted, hands on her back, Pa's head bent, wincing.

Look up, Clancy. Look up.

Nan's voice was so clear, the scent of lily-of-the-valley so strong, that she was sure the others must have heard it, too.

Look up, Clancy! See the moon?

She looked up, into the deep blue late afternoon sky. But she couldn't see the moon.

What do you mean, Nan? What moon?

A flash of colour in the corner of her eye made her turn her head. Pip's battered old car carried a sticker in the back window, a circular gold and blue medieval-looking symbol, half sun, half moon-face.

See the moon, Clancy?

And in a flash, she knew.

Pip and Tash were arguing about the taxi now, each brandishing a phone like a weapon. Clancy interrupted. 'Would we fit in Pip's car?'

'Ha!' snorted Pip. 'I don't know if you've noticed, but I'm extremely pregnant? I can't reach the pedals anymore. I can't even drive to the shops, definitely not all the way to Rosella.'

There was a brief silence.

Then Toby said, 'But I can.'

'No way,' said Pip and Tash together, and glared at each other.

'We have to!' said Clancy, surprising herself with the firmness of her tone. 'We don't have time to wait for a taxi. Poor Pa needs his medication.'

'I don't think—' began Tash, but Clancy spoke over her.

'We can't waste time arguing. And Toby knows how to drive. I've seen him. Let's just go!'

In the end, it was Clancy who hustled them all into the car. Having hastily slapped his L-plates on the car, Toby took the driver's seat, nervous but determined, adjusting the mirrors and the seat. Pip clambered in laboriously beside him, checking the route on her phone and complaining bitterly. 'Better take the inland road, with a learner – it's boring but it's easier. I cannot believe I'm actually doing this...I must be insane...'

With Clancy and Toby's assistance, Pa managed to shuffle himself painfully into the middle of the back seat, while Tash folded down the wheelchair and shoved it into the boot, which didn't shut properly and had to be secured with an occy strap. At last Tash hurled herself into the back seat and slammed the door, which made Pa and Pip both wince.

Toby looked into the rear-view mirror for confirmation. 'Ready?'

Tash was busy with her seatbelt, and Pa's eyes were closed, so it was Clancy who answered, 'Yes. Let's go.'

Toby turned the key in the ignition, the engine coughed, and Pip said, 'Don't forget the handbrake.'

'I know, I know.' Toby's face was very white as he turned to make a head check before backing out of the driveway; but his face was always pale.

As she sat in the back of the car holding one of Pa's hands while Tash cradled the other, Clancy thought she glimpsed just a wink of bright light in the sky outside the window. But perhaps it was only an aeroplane.

38

As soon as they were clear of Cockatoo Bay and safely out onto the open road, Pip punched a number into her phone.

'Who are you calling?' asked Tash in alarm.

'Polly.' Pip pressed the phone to her ear. 'She started the manhunt, she can be the one to call it off— Yeah, Poll? It's me. I've got them... Yeah, all three. All fine... No, I'm in the car... No, to Rosella. To get Dad's meds... Because they were left there... How the hell should I know? I suppose they left in a hurry. Poll, I can't talk. I'm supervising a learner driver... No, not Tash... *I don't know.* I'm going, I'm going... Yeah, you too.' She hung up with a sniff and turned to Toby. 'Put your foot down, buster. You're slower than a wet week. You can do a hundred along here.'

'I haven't gone that fast yet.' Toby peered over the steering wheel at the road ahead. 'I've never been on a freeway.'

'Are people on their L-plates allowed to drive that fast?' said Clancy.

Pip snorted. 'Of course they can! It's more dangerous to go *slower* than the limit on the freeway.'

'I don't think that's right,' Toby said. The car jerked forward as he put his foot down. 'Sorry! Sorry, sorry.'

'You're right,' grunted Pip. 'Just keep going.'

Toby muttered something that Clancy couldn't hear. She could see his knuckles clutched white around the wheel, and she realised that he was terrified. Admiration leapt up inside her like a firework.

They drove.

'Can't we put on some music or something?' complained Tash.

'Do you mind if we don't?' said Toby. 'I need to concentrate.'

Tash glanced across to Clancy and rolled her eyes, but Clancy frowned. She thought Toby was amazing.

'Sp-sp-sp,' grumbled Pa. He tried to stretch out his left leg, but there wasn't room. 'Sp-sp!' He shifted around on his bum.

'Do you need the bottle?' asked Tash, almost hopefully, Clancy thought – anything to break the monotony. But Pa shook his head. After a while, his head lolled forward and he began to snore.

'Hey, Pip—' began Tash, but Clancy caught her sister's eye, pointed to Toby, and shook her head. *Don't talk while he's driving.*

Tash opened her mouth to argue, then closed it again, and shrugged.

'Yeah, what?' said Pip.

'Never mind. Nothing.'

'Pip?' said Clancy, after a moment.

'What now?'

'Maybe you should call Bee. I think she's going to be worried about us, too.'

'You guys have really left a trail of destruction, haven't you?' said Pip.

'Also—' Clancy swallowed. 'She's not in the city. She lives on an ashram now.'

'*What*?' Pip twisted round.

'Clancy! We promised!' cried Tash.

'Ssh!' said Toby. 'Please.'

Pip shook her head. 'I'm speechless,' she said; but she left a message at the ashram anyway.

They drove along the freeway, through the same yellow paddocks that they'd seen from the train – was it really only yesterday? – past fences and silos, dead trees and sheep. Clancy found herself sitting tensely upright, watching the road over Toby's shoulder. There was a truck in front of them; as it laboured up a hill, Clancy watched it draw closer...actually it was their car that was coming nearer as the truck slowed down—

'Watch it!' said Pip sharply. 'Slow down, slow down! Jesus!'

She flung out one hand to the dashboard as Toby hit

the brakes and they were all thrown forward, brought up hard by their seatbelts. Pa grunted, but kept on snoring.

'Sorry!'

The gap between Pip's car and the truck stretched out again as Toby slowed down. Someone tooted, then there was a rush of wind as the car behind them overtook, racing past and swerving into the gap. Toby flinched.

Pip muttered something under her breath.

As they passed a sign for an approaching service station, Clancy realised, *Toby needs a break. But he doesn't want to say so, in case Pip and Tash think he's a wuss. But what if he crashes? Or what if he just stops the car and says,* That's it, I can't take it anymore? *What would we do then?*

Nervously she leaned forward. 'Pip? I need the toilet. Can we stop up here?'

Even before Pip said, 'Yeah, okay,' Toby was already pulling across into the exit lane.

When Clancy returned from the toilet, Tash was leaning against the car. She tore open a packet of chips and passed the bag to Clancy. Pa was still asleep in the back seat. Pip had passed Clancy as she swayed off to the toilet, and Toby had said he was going, too, but Clancy could see him pacing up and down the concourse, shaking out his stiff hands and legs.

'Hey, Clance,' said Tash, after a few moments of munching.

Clancy steeled herself. What had she done wrong now?

'I was just going to tell you—'

Here we go...

'—I was going to say it before, but I got distracted – just that, you know, I'm glad you came along.'

Clancy blinked. 'Seriously?'

'Yeah, seriously. You're observant. You notice stuff. You're really good at that.'

'Thanks,' said Clancy cautiously.

'Now you say what I'm best at.' Tash held out her hand for the chip packet.

'Oh – thinking up plans. Arguing. Getting stuff done.'

'I was kidding, but thanks anyway.'

Clancy gently punched her sister's arm. 'Ha-ha.'

'Seriously, though – we're a pretty good team, I reckon, you and me.'

'I think so, too,' said Clancy shyly.

'And hey – don't worry about high school. You'll be fine. Turns out you're better at making friends than I thought you were.' Tash grabbed a handful of chips and stuffed them in her mouth, pulling a funny face at the same time so that Clancy could laugh at her and not need to answer.

After a moment, Clancy said, 'I'm sad all this didn't work out. You know, for Pa.'

'Yeah,' said Tash. 'Me too.'

'At least we tried.'

'Yeah. We did.'

They stood by the car, munching quietly. Behind them, the setting sun stained the sky with orange flames. Up ahead, on the eastern horizon, a streak of silver light flashed across the dark blue sky. Clancy gasped, and clutched Tash's arm.

'Did you see that?'

'I saw *something*,' said Tash doubtfully. 'I think it was a helicopter.'

'No, it wasn't! Come on, Tash, it was a meteor. It was a sign, from Nan!'

'Not this again,' groaned Tash.

'What's that about Nan?' Pip loomed up out of the shadows and plunged her hand into the chip packet. 'You wouldn't even remember Nan, would you, Clancy?'

'I do remember her,' said Clancy. 'She loved stars.'

'Yeah, that's right, she did.' Pip sounded surprised.

'Clancy's obsessed with space,' said Tash. 'For some reason.'

'I ended up with your nan's telescope,' said Pip. 'But I never use it. Stars aren't my thing, I'm more of a surfer chick, you know?'

'I'd wondered what happened to that telescope!' said Clancy.

Pip helped herself to the last crumbs from the chip packet. 'Well, if you're into all that space stuff, you should have it. If you want.'

Clancy was speechless.

'She'd love it,' said Tash kindly. 'She says, "thanks, Pip, that would be awesome". Don't you, peanut?'

'Thanks, Pip,' whispered Clancy.

'No worries.' Pip brushed the salt from her finger-tips. 'Where's our chauffeur gone? Hey, Toby!' she yelled across the concourse. 'Ready to go?'

As Toby jogged back, and Tash and Pip climbed into the car, Clancy paused for a moment to glance overhead.

One by one, the stars were coming out. But that wasn't right, she reminded herself; the stars were always there. They were just being revealed, as the last sunlight drained from the dark blue bowl of the sky, leaving a trail of spilled glitter behind, a glimmer of gold in the bottom of the pan. All those ancient patterns and stories, turning in the sky, spelled out in a language Clancy couldn't read.

But when she had a telescope, she could learn to read it...

Clancy gave a little skip, and dived back inside the car.

39

By the time the car crawled up the hills to the house in Rosella, the sky was black and Nan's moon was shining high and bright and small, like a torchlight leading them through the night.

'Turn right here,' said Pip. 'This is the street. Second driveway on the right... What's with the *For Sale* sign?'

'Yeah, I want to talk to Polly about that,' muttered Tash darkly.

'You're not the only one,' said Pip indignantly. 'Just because she's got power of attorney, she thinks she can do whatever she likes. She can't sell our childhood home without even *consulting* us! Just wait till I speak to her—'

'Looks like you won't have to wait long,' said Tash. 'She's here.'

The headlights swept over the driveway, lighting up Polly's little red car parked in the carport. Carefully Toby inched along between the bushes, braked, put the car into park, and switched off the engine. He dropped his forehead onto the steering wheel, breathing hard.

'Lights,' said Pip, releasing her seatbelt.

Toby fumbled the headlights off, and let his head drop back on the steering wheel. Tash was already scrambling out of the car. Clancy couldn't move; she had Pa's head resting on her shoulder.

'Toby?' she said anxiously. 'You okay?'

'Yeah – yeah, I think so.' He groped for the doorhandle and eased it open, then swung his legs out of the car. He seemed to need to take his exit in stages. Even after he climbed out of the driver's seat, he just leaned against the side of the car. He turned to give Clancy a wobbly grin. 'My knees are shaking.'

'That was a big drive!' said Clancy.

'Yeah.' Toby perked up slightly. 'It's going to look great in my logbook.'

By this time, Pip had heaved herself out of the car and waddled over to Polly by the front door. 'Hey, sis.'

Polly looked Pip up and down. 'You've been busy, I see.'

'Oh, here it comes...'

The two sisters glared at each other in the light that blazed from the windows and the open door. Tash called, 'Did you find Pa's pills, Polly?'

'Yes, I did, and I've got some questions for you, young lady. Where's your grandfather?'

'He's in the car!' called Clancy, opening her door. She shook Pa gently. 'Time to wake up, Pa – we're home.'

Pa gazed blearily toward the house, and his face lit up with bewildered joy when he realised where they were. Clancy could have kicked herself. Why did she have to say *home*, and get his hopes up, when he'd just be going back to The Elms again? All their hard work, all their plans, their traipsing around all over the state, had been for nothing: that was disappointing enough for Clancy and Tash, but how much worse would it be for Pa?

Clancy slid out of the car and let Polly and Tash manoeuvre Pa out of the back seat. He clung tightly to Tash, moaning and swaying, his eyes squeezed shut. They had to lower him gently down into the chair and bend his knees and ankles; he was as stiff as wood, and every movement seemed to hurt him.

He'll need water to take the pills, thought Clancy, *but there aren't any cups here.* She grabbed the water bottle from Tash's backpack and sprinted inside to fill it.

Squabbling and jostling one another, Pip and Polly and Tash squeezed through the front door and into the empty living room, pushing Pa ahead of them. Toby followed slowly, and stood hesitating just inside the doorway, as if he wasn't sure whether or not he was really welcome inside.

Clancy found the pills in their little plastic packet on the sink where Polly had left them. Carefully she tipped them out onto her palm and went to kneel beside her grandfather.

'Pa? Here's your medication. And some water to wash it down.'

Pa blinked at her and slowly raised his shaking hand. 'Aargh!' He cursed as he knocked the pills to the carpet.

'It's okay. I'll help.' Clancy picked up the pills and popped the first one onto Pa's tongue. She waited for him to swallow a mouthful of water from the bottle, then nod when he was ready for the next one. At last they were all gone, and Pa breathed a deep sigh. Pip and Polly and Tash were still arguing and explaining and contradicting each other, standing under the living room light as if it were a spotlight.

Pa patted Clancy's shoulder and pointed to the front windows as two lights swung around the street corner and lit up the driveway. Toby peered through the front door.

'It's a cab,' he reported. 'It's stopping here...It's a man and a woman, and a boy.'

Clancy gave a strangled cry and pushed past him to fly up the driveway and into Tim's arms.

Adding Bruno, Tim and Harriet into the echoing living room doubled the volume of excited voices. Even Toby was drawn into the hubbub, stammering a muddled explanation of who he was and what he was doing there. Tim accused Polly, 'How could you go off and leave them like that? What were you thinking?'; Polly had begun to cry; Bruno was charging around the empty rooms, shouting something about the bush and firemen and New Zealand at the top of his voice; Harriet was calling for order; Tash stamped her foot and cried, 'Listen! You're not *listening* to me!'

Pa was sitting off to one side of the room. His eyes were closed, but his skin looked pinker, and less grey, Clancy thought, and his face looked more peaceful, not screwed up in pain. She touched his arm.

'Pa? Are you feeling any better?'

Without opening his eyes, Pa nodded. He flicked his hand and Clancy understood. *Yes, I'm all right, but I'd like to be left alone.* She dropped a kiss on top of his fluffy head and stepped back toward the glass doors to the deck. It was dark out there...dark and quiet. Unnoticed, Clancy slid the door open and slipped outside into the night.

Out on the deck, with the door closed behind her, everything was quiet. The just-past-full moon sailed high above the dark bulk of the mountain, and the ragged silhouettes of the treetops were outlined against the sky. Leaves rustled as an unseen possum swarmed along the branch, and a cool breeze brushed Clancy's cheek as she leaned on the railing and breathed in deeply, smelling the fresh scent of eucalyptus.

The stars were much clearer out here at Rosella than they were in the city, like tiny chips of diamond thickly sprinkled across the sky. Clancy picked out the Southern Cross, the pointers, the three brothers in their canoe from the Yolgnu story; but the other stars were a mystery. Were the seven sisters up there somewhere? The planets? Maybe she could sneak her book out here and search for the constellations of the January sky. It would be even easier if she had Nan's telescope...

Even as she watched, the moon seemed to rise higher above the trees. The moon, the earth's silent, smaller sister, pulled together out of dust and rock into this magical silver companion... Clancy smiled, remembering Toby's theory about gravity being the enemy of entropy.

When Clancy turned around and looked back through the glass into the house, she could see almost all of Dad's family, except for Mark and Bee, gathered in the living room, all talking at once, animated, waving their arms around, interrupting one another. It looked like a happy family reunion, thought Clancy wistfully, if you didn't know how angry they all were.

When was the last time they had all been together in one room? She didn't know. Some Christmas dinner, maybe, years ago? Or perhaps when Pa was in hospital after his stroke, and they'd all been scared he was going to die? Clancy hadn't realised until this moment that she could even remember that, but now a sharp-edged image returned to her: sliding along a hard vinyl couch in a waiting room with Bruno and Tash while the adults clustered around a hospital bed. And Bruno had crashed off the couch and split his head open on a coffee table – a sudden vivid flash of memory, the shocking scarlet flower of blood on her brother's forehead—

And now here they were again. Except that this time, it was Nan who had brought them all together. The gravitational power of Nan's magic, working against the entropy of the family drifting in their separate directions.

Clancy's heart gave a sudden thump. Was this what Nan had wanted all this time? For the separate rocks and dust of everybody to merge together into one clump of family?

But not like this. Not arguing, not shouting at each other, with no one listening. Not with Pa sitting sadly off to one side, his eyes closed, his head bowed on his chest. *Look up, Pa!* Clancy silently urged him. *Everyone's here! Look up!*

Look up at the sky, Clancy. See the moon?

Nan's voice whispered in her mind. Clancy tipped back her head to gaze at the stars. And all at once, she knew what she had to do.

40

Before she could give herself a chance to think, Clancy wrenched open the glass doors and rushed inside.

'I know what we should do!' she cried. 'I've got the answer!'

Every face turned, startled, to stare at her. Even Pa jerked awake and gazed up, confused. Bruno skidded to a halt in the hallway and watched her, wide-eyed.

'Clancy—' began Harriet.

But Tash spoke over her mother. 'Come on, peanut,' she said. 'Tell us your big idea.'

'Okay...' Clancy stopped. Pa, Tash, Tim, Harriet, Bruno, Polly, Pip and Toby were waiting, eight sets of eyes all fixed on her. Could she convince them? She suddenly felt very small and very alone.

Clancy breathed in, and the scent of lily-of-the-valley filled her nostrils. She wasn't alone after all.

'We've been acting like Pa is the moon,' said Clancy slowly, working out her words as she spoke. 'He's just been kind of off to the side—' She saw Polly beginning to open her mouth to object, and hurried on, '—but why shouldn't he be a star?'

'What *are* you talking about?' said Tash. But she said it kindly.

Clancy went to stand behind her grandfather and laid her hands on his shoulders.

'What if we moved in here?' she said.

'What the hell does that have to do with stars and moons?' began Pip, but Tim put up his hand for her to stop.

'Move in here, to this house?' he said. 'You want to live in Rosella?'

'Impossible!' said Harriet briskly.

But this time Clancy wasn't going to give in so easily. 'We could live here,' she persisted. 'There are loads of bedrooms. And Pa could live here, too.'

'Ah!' breathed Pa softly, and he reached up and covered Clancy's hand with his own.

'But Clancy,' said Tim gently. 'I don't think you realise just how much looking after Pa needs.'

Clancy drew herself up straight and tall. 'Yes, I do. Tash and I have been taking care of him all weekend.'

'Yeah,' said Tash. 'It's not *that* hard.'

'Apart from remembering his medication!' said Polly.

Tash shrugged. 'So, we forgot one thing. We won't do it again. Lesson learned. Big deal, move on.'

'But darling—' said Harriet.

'Sp-sp-sp,' said Pa suddenly. He held up five fingers then two, pointed to himself, and gestured around him. 'Sp-sp-sp!'

'There are five of us to look after him,' said Tash.

'Nah, nah!' Pa held up five fingers, and pointed over his shoulder, then held up two fingers, and jabbed toward the floor. 'Sp-sp-sp!'

'Five pills?' guessed Polly.

'Five days?' suggested Toby, from the door.

'Weekdays!' said Clancy, inspired. 'You can stay at The Elms during the week, and live here with us at the weekends.'

'Yes!' roared Pa. 'So-it-is, yes!'

There was a brief silence.

At last Harriet said carefully, 'Living out here is a lovely idea. But how would I get to work?'

'You could catch the train,' said Clancy stubbornly. 'And Rosella is closer to Dad's school than where we live now.'

'That's true, actually.' Tim shot a quick look at Harriet. 'But what about school for you guys?'

'I don't mind commuting,' offered Tash. 'Turns out I really like trains. And I could stay over with Az or Miranda sometimes. It'd be cool. Like going to uni.'

Tim shook his head. 'Clancy can't commute all that way. Not in her very first year of high school. It's too much.'

Toby cleared his throat. 'If you guys did move here, Clancy could go to Tutt's Flat College.'

Tim, Harriet, Tash and Clancy turned to stare at him. Toby flushed. 'I know kids who go there. It's a good school.'

'Well,' said Harriet, 'thank you for your input – Toby, is it? But I believe this is a family discussion.'

Toby's flush spread to the tips of his ears. 'Sorry.'

'He's right, though,' said Tim. 'Tutt's Flat has a pretty good rep.'

'You're all forgetting something,' said Polly, slightly shrill. 'This house is for sale. We need the money to pay for The Elms.'

'Let's buy it then!' cried Bruno. 'I like this house. It's awesome. I want my own room. No offence, Clance,' he added. 'But when we were in New Zealand, I had my own room and...yeah, it was pretty cool.'

'Living here would be good for Bruno,' said Tash persuasively. 'He'd be running round the garden instead of locked inside, staring at a screen.'

Clancy suppressed a grin. She knew this was a sore point with their parents.

'While I appreciate your concern for your brother's physical and mental health,' said Harriet drily, 'we don't have that much spare cash lying around. We'd have to sell our apartment.'

'The apartment would be worth more than this house,' said Tim, almost to himself. 'We'd have money left over...'

Clancy and Tash flashed glances.

'Tim!' exclaimed Harriet. 'Are you actually taking this crazy notion seriously?'

Pip leaned against a wall and lowered herself cautiously to the floor. 'Wake me up when you've sorted it out, will you? My back is killing me.'

'Never mind your back. Let's take Dad home,' said Polly. 'He must be exhausted.'

'Sp-sp-sp!' protested Pa.

'He's feeling heaps better,' said Clancy.

'And he wants to know what we're going to decide,' said Tash.

'We'll talk about it tomorrow,' said Tim firmly.

'Woo-hoo!' yelled Bruno. 'I bags the green room!'

'Bruno! Nothing's been decided yet,' said Harriet sharply.

But Clancy and Tash were exchanging looks of wild hope. If they were both keen…and Pa was keen…and Bruno was keen…and Tim was taking it seriously… their mother was beaten already, even if she didn't know it yet.

'Well, now we've got ten people and a wheelchair to fit into two cars,' said Tim. 'Not very big cars, either.'

'Nine people,' said Polly.

'What?' Tim glanced around the room. 'You're right, nine. Where did I get ten from?'

There was a snort from Pip, leaning against the wall with her eyes closed. 'Call yourself a teacher! No wonder the education system's in trouble.'

But Clancy, looking out toward the night, had seen their reflections in the glass. Just for a second, she thought she glimpsed the shadowy figure of a woman standing beside Pa's wheelchair; and she knew why her father had counted wrong.

41

Clancy dropped her Tutt's Flat Secondary College schoolbag by the front door (Tim would later growl at her for leaving it there), kicked off her runners and followed her nose to the kitchen where fresh Anzac biscuits were cooling on a tray.

'Don't touch those,' warned Polly, stacking the dishwasher. 'They're for your pa.'

'Don't worry, I'm not a massive fan of Anzacs,' Clancy assured her. 'They smell good, but, you know – coconut. Blerch. No offence,' she added hastily.

Polly looked surprised, but not as annoyed as Clancy feared she might be. 'Well, that's just un-Australian,' was all she said. Perhaps they'd been wrong about Polly, and she did have a sense of humour after all. 'How was school?'

'Good. There was a meeting after school about the astronomy camp later in the year. I *really* want to go.'

'Sounds like fun,' said Polly politely.

Clancy lolled against the bench. 'What were you into when you were at school, Polly?'

Polly laughed. 'Would you believe, musical theatre? I starred in *West Side Story*. I was *amazing*. I'll bring my videos next Friday and show you.' Polly struck a pose, beaming nostalgically.

'Wow,' said Clancy, stunned. 'Can I put your videos on YouTube? The Dancing Dentist?'

'Absolutely not,' said Polly, picking up her keys. 'I'll be off now. You'll be right till your dad comes home?'

'Of course,' said Clancy.

'You could take some bikkies out to Pa and Bruno,' suggested Polly as she headed for the door.

'Theoretically, I could,' agreed Clancy. 'But the question is, can I be bothered?'

'Oh!' Polly paused at the threshold. 'I forgot – a parcel came for you. It's on the dining table.'

Feels like a textbook, thought Clancy, as she ripped open the packaging. There was no return address on the wrapping, nor a sticker to show its origin. But when Clancy pulled the heavy book from its bubble wrap, she felt a shock of recognition. It was the star atlas of the southern sky that she'd found at The Magpie Bookshop.

Clancy hugged the book to her chest; it was solid and weighty and definitely real. It was a full stop at the end of the magic.

After a few moments, she laid the book on the table to be savoured later. She dutifully piled a plate with warm biscuits and carried them, past the corner where Nan's telescope was nestled, out onto the deck where her brother and grandfather sat side by side, absorbed in one of Pa's bird books.

Bruno looked up. 'Hey, Clance! Pa's helping me with my bird list. I started it with Mark in New Zealand. Did I tell you about the time I got lost in the bush there and the fire brigade had to rescue me?'

'Only about a gazillion times,' said Clancy kindly.

'Sp-sp-sp.' Pa tapped his finger on the cover of his own bird book and flipped it open to show Clancy a page of cockatoos.

'Cockatoo Bay?' Clancy gasped. 'Did Pip have her baby?'

'No, no, no,' said Pa impatiently.

'Pip's never going to have that damn baby,' groaned Bruno.

'It's not even due yet,' said Clancy. 'Not till next week.'

'A-hem!' Pa coughed for her attention. 'Sp-sp.' He pointed to his binoculars, then to the tallest gum tree.

'We saw a cockatoo, but we can't decide if it's a glossy black cockatoo or a red-tailed cockatoo,' said Bruno. 'We're waiting for it to come back.'

'That's nice,' said Clancy absently, then laughed as she recognised the echo of Polly's bland reaction to her own excitement about astronomy camp. People were different; they were into different things. It was just the way the world was; you couldn't do anything about it. It could be fun when your interests overlapped with somebody's else's, like she and Toby with astronomy, or Bee and Nan with yoga, or Pa and Bruno and Mark with birds, or Tim and Tash with football. But Clancy was never going to be interested in football, and she was never going to be the same as Tash. And Clancy was cool with that.

On the other hand, she was changing, a little at a time. Starting a new school hadn't been as terrifying as she'd expected. Much to her father's delight, she'd begun reading more books. And slowly, one step at a time, she was teaching herself other things.

She jumped up. 'I'm going to make a pudding in a mug. Anyone else want one?'

Pa bit into an Anzac biscuit and shook his head.

'Are you *cooking*?' said Bruno.

'It's barely cooking,' said Clancy. 'But if you don't want one...'

'I didn't say *that*,' said Bruno.

As Clancy spooned cocoa, self-raising flour and sugar into two mugs, she remembered how Antonia had shown them how to make puddings. Their visit to The Magpie Bookshop seemed like years ago. But she felt *much* older now than she had then. And she was pretty sure that she was taller, too.

Clancy stirred through the milk, and put the mugs into the microwave. As she stood waiting for the puddings to cook, she glanced through the window at the deck, and saw a large, black-feathered bird alight on the rail.

Pa and Bruno were frozen, gazing intently at it. Pa reached out his hand, palm flat, with the last morsel of

Anzac biscuit. The black cockatoo sidled up and pecked it from his hand. Bruno let out a shout of delight. The cockatoo squinted a disapproving look at him, and ponderously flapped away.

Pa twisted around to see if Clancy had witnessed this triumph, and gave her a thumbs-up, beaming. *If only Nan could see him now!* thought Clancy, as she returned his signal; *but maybe she can.*

42

The microwave pinged, and Clancy jumped. She took out the steaming mugs. Was there cream in the fridge? Why, yes, there was. She carried the puddings out to the deck, and that was where Tash found them when she arrived home a few minutes later.

'Yum, Anzacs!' She'd grabbed a handful from the rack on the bench. 'Polly?'

'Well, it wasn't me.' Clancy dug her spoon into her pudding.

Tash stretched out her legs on the sun-warmed planks of the deck and munched contentedly. Pa patted his stomach and let out a satisfied belch, which made Bruno laugh, and Tash and Clancy groan in disgust.

'Hey, Tash! We saw a black cockatoo!'

'Yeah? Good for you.'

'Can't wait to tell Mark,' said Bruno with satisfaction.

'Sp-sp-sp,' agreed Pa.

Tash squinted up at them. 'You know Mark's dating one of the staff from The Elms now?'

'No way!' squealed Clancy. 'Not Belinda!'

Tash shuddered. 'No, not Belinda. One of the nice ones.'

'How do you know?'

'I heard Polly telling Dad. She is such a gossip. Mark brought them home for dinner the other night.'

'Sp-sp-sp?' asked Pa, agog.

'I don't know who. But I'll find out.'

Harriet had succeeded in getting Mark released, and he'd come back to Australia, rather less wild than before. He was living with Polly until he found a job and a place of his own. Polly grumbled about it, but Clancy thought she was secretly enjoying having a housemate. Mark would be fun to live with.

It was a sunny autumn afternoon. They'd agreed to buy the house and moved to Rosella in a hectic rush just before the start of term. Clancy was still trying to get used to the sight of their own familiar furniture sitting in Pa's house. A few boxes they hadn't had time to unpack yet were piled in corners. When Pa visited, he'd point to them and raise his eyebrows at their slack attitude and they would all look back innocently and pretend they didn't understand.

Clancy and Tash had chosen the big pink bedroom. Part of the deal they'd hammered out with Tim and Harriet was that they would share a bedroom, so Pa could have one of his own. But this room was much larger than either of their old ones, so it was worth it. They were still debating whether to paint the walls purple, like the back room of The Magpie Bookshop; or terracotta and green, like the dormitories at Bee's ashram; or white with cherry trim, like the Breakfast in Kyoto café. Clancy had argued for a black ceiling with stars and planets, but Tash had vetoed that. So for the moment, it was still pink.

Pa was living with them part-time. He spent most of the week at The Elms, and came to stay at Rosella at weekends, ferried by Sidhu the taxi driver. It turned out that Neneh had been joking when she'd threatened that Belinda would expel Pa from The Elms. They had been hugely relieved and pleased to see him again, and some of the staff had even cried, which was a massive ego boost for Pa. (Clancy hoped it was Neneh that Mark was dating; she really liked Neneh.)

There was still some complicated money stuff to sort out, but Tim and Harriet and Polly were working on it. Polly had rearranged her week so that she could spend Fridays with Pa at Rosella. Usually he stayed for the weekend, and the family would drive to the park, or to watch Tash play footy, or just spend time in the garden or on the deck, birdwatching. On clear nights, Clancy was making good use of Nan's old telescope. Bruno was lobbying for a dog. Harriet had cut back her work hours, and sometimes she worked from home. Tash said their mother had got a fright, seeing what had happened to Mark in New Zealand. 'Her theory is he went off the rails because Nan and Pa didn't spend enough time with him. Apparently.'

'But he seems okay now,' said Clancy. 'And how did Dad and Polly and Bee and Pip turn out so well?'

'You think Polly turned out well?' said Tash automatically; but she didn't mean it. Polly, like most people, was improving on closer acquaintance.

Perhaps it was a coincidence that they'd caught Harriet at a vulnerable moment with Clancy's grand plan (Plan D, as she and Tash called it, though no one else apart from Toby and Pa knew why). Or perhaps that was Nan's magic at work again.

Bee had been cross at first that Clancy had told everyone about the ashram, but to her surprise no one had particularly minded. 'It's your life,' shrugged Pip. 'If I can have a baby on my own, why shouldn't you stand on your head all day if you want to?'

'Not all day,' said Bee. 'Just sometimes.'

Clancy was relieved that neither she nor Tash had been sent to prison for kidnapping their grandfather, although the local sergeant had given them a talk about *wasting police resources* and *letting people know next time, okay?*

And the new spirit of family had extended itself to Harriet. She'd called her mother and her brothers for the first time for ages, and there was talk of Po Po coming down from Sydney for a visit sometime.

Now Clancy said, 'Hey, Tash. Come here, I want to show you something.'

43

Inside, Tash picked up the star atlas and turned it over in her hands. 'Wow,' she said, after a long pause.

'It's the one I found at Antonia's bookshop,' said Clancy.

'Yeah, I remember. And this arrived today? That is truly bizarre.' Tash put down the book and leaned in. 'You know I had an excursion to the city today? I thought I'd drop in and say hi to Antonia, tell her about Pa and moving and everything—'

'But the bookshop disappeared. The arcade disappeared – everything.'

'And I didn't believe you,' admitted Tash. 'Or maybe deep down I did believe you, but I didn't want to. Anyway, I went looking today...' She pulled out her ponytail and retied it. 'And yeah, you were right. It was gone.'

'I told you!' said Clancy.

'So then I looked up The Magpie Bookshop on the internet and it came up as permanently closed.'

'Did you look up Antonia Wildwood?'

Tash screwed up her face. 'I don't really want to. I'm a bit scared of what I might find. What if it says she died five years ago or something? That's too spooky for me.' She touched the book. 'But if she is dead, then where did this come from?'

'I don't know,' said Clancy.

They were silent for a moment.

'You want to know something else weird?' said Tash. 'You know how I was pushing Pa around everywhere, all over the city, and up and down hills and out at Quoll Creek?'

'Yes...'

'Well, when I try to push him up the street now, I can hardly do it. It's like, *really* hard! Even if it's only a little slope – it's like pushing an elephant over a wall. So what's that all about? It's not like I could have got *less* strong.'

'Maybe Nan was helping you?' said Clancy.

Tash pulled a face. 'Yeah, right.'

'Why not?'

'But – how?'

They stared at each other.

'Magic?' said Clancy.

'That's just another way of saying *I don't understand*,' said Tash. 'That doesn't explain anything.'

'I told you Nan was helping us out, showing us where to go. Maybe she was helping you to push Pa, too. Maybe she opened up a wormhole or something so we could go back in time and visit Antonia.' Clancy clutched her sister's arm. 'You know that podcast, *The Grandfather Paradox*—'

Tash smirked. 'The one Toby told you about?'

'Yes – whatever – the other day they were talking about pocket universes, and multiple universes. I couldn't really understand it, but what if Nan made a little pocket in time, so that Pa could see Antonia one more time and say goodbye?'

'So now you're saying Nan's ghost created a whole universe, so that we could hang out with an old friend of hers? I'm not buying it.'

'Or maybe we just went back in time.'

'*Just!* Oh, yeah, that's a much simpler theory.'

'Have you got a better one?' demanded Clancy.

'No,' said Tash crossly.

'Maybe it's better not to think about it too hard,' said Clancy. 'I mean, if you can explain magic, then it's not magic anymore.'

'Pfft!' Tash flipped her hand, imitating Pa. 'Nan's ghost, Antonia's ghost, we went back in time, it's all crazy. But I did it, you did it, Pa did it. We've got the evidence. We've got those books, and now this one, too. We can't all be mad... Speaking of, have you seen Nan's ghost hanging around since we moved in? Any more of your spooky signs?'

Clancy shook her head. 'No, nothing. But hey, we're here, Pa's here, the whole family is talking to each other again. Maybe it's all worked out the way she wanted, so she's gone.'

'Personally, I'm okay with that.' Tash wrinkled her nose. 'I'm not a hundred per cent comfortable with the idea of a ghost creeping round our house.'

'Not even Nan?' said Clancy wistfully.

'Not even Nan.'

There was a small pause, then Tash heaved her school-bag onto her back. 'Well, some of us have homework.'

'So that's what you call playing music and watching movies on your phone?' said Clancy.

'Your turn will come,' said Tash ominously. 'One day you're going to have so much homework that you'll need to take a little break occasionally, just for your own sanity. You're lucky to have me to help and advise you.'

'I so cannot wait to reap the benefit of your wisdom,' said Clancy.

They grinned at each other in a friendly way, then Tash loped off to their bedroom. Clancy stayed in the dining room, hugging the star atlas close to her.

It was sad to think that Antonia might be dead. Or was she still alive in a parallel, pocket universe? Maybe, one day, Clancy might be able to wriggle back into it and say *thanks for everything*. Or perhaps Antonia was hanging out with Nan, two ghostly friends together? Clancy didn't mind that idea.

She sighed. She had the star atlas to explore, and a good view of Saturn tonight. There were some kids at her new school who seemed like they might become friends, and she had a text from Toby on her new phone to reply to. Astronomy camp. A new baby in the family, the possibility of a dog, and Pa looking happier every day.

Yes, decided Clancy as she gathered the wrappings from the parcel. There was a lot to look forward to.

ACKNOWLEDGEMENTS

Thank you to Dr Duane Hamacher, Associate Professor of Indigenous Astronomy & Science at the University of Melbourne, and to Sophie Splatt, Jodie Webster and Eva Mills at Allen & Unwin.

ABOUT THE AUTHOR

Kate Constable was born in Melbourne but spent much of her childhood in Papua New Guinea, without television but within reach of a library where she 'inhaled' stories. She studied Arts/Law at the University of Melbourne before working for a record company while she began her life as a writer. Kate had stories published in *Meanjin*, *Island* and other literary magazines before realising she was actually a children's and YA author. Kate has written ten novels for young people, including the internationally published Chanters of Tremaris series and the CBCA award-winning *Crow Country*. Kate lives in a northern suburb of Melbourne with her family, a bearded dragon, a rabbit and a dog.

AUTHOR'S NOTE

Authors are always being asked, 'Where do you get your ideas from?' For *The January Stars*, the answer is easy. The initial inspiration for this story came from my own family. Several years ago, my father, Bill – my children's papa – had a severe stroke on the left side of his brain. At first, his right side was completely paralysed and he was unable to speak, write or remember numbers or the alphabet. When I began to write *The January Stars*, I made the character of Pa more independent than Bill was at the time, but now Bill has caught up! After a lot of hard work and rehabilitation, he can walk short distances, though he still uses a wheelchair. Bill might not be able to speak, but he can express himself in other ways and his stubborn, determined character is as vivid as ever. In this book, I was interested in exploring how family relationships can still survive and even thrive despite the devastation of stroke and aphasia. The biggest difference between the novel and real life is that my wonderful mother, Jan, is still very much alive and a vital part of Bill's daily life.

Sadie isn't thrilled when her mother drags her from the city to live in the country town of Boort. But soon she starts making connections – connections with the country, with the past, with two boys, Lachie and Walter, and, most surprisingly, with the ever-present crows. When Sadie is tumbled back in time to view a terrible crime, she is pulled into a strange mystery. Can Sadie, Walter and Lachie figure out a way to right old wrongs, or will they be condemned to repeat them?

———————

WINNER: CBCA Book of the Year, Younger Readers, 2012

'*Crow Country* is a book that sweeps you deliciously off your feet into a world where you feel immediately at home; with Kate Constable you know you are in safe hands. A thoroughly enjoyable read. Highly recommended.' *Magpies*

'*Crow Country* is a novel that readers will dive straight into and devour…' *Bookseller + Publisher*

'The text is evocative, the characters are sympathetic and the story is absorbing.' *Good Reading*

'Sometimes you read a book and you don't want it to end. For me, *Crow Country* was such a book.' *Ballarat Courier*

Crow
Country

Kate
Constable

When Eloise's get-rich-quick dad moves them back to his home town to turn the derelict family mansion into a convention centre, Eloise feels an immediate bond with the old house. She begins spending all her time there, ignoring her strange grandmother and avoiding the friendly boy next door. Then Eloise meets a 'ghost girl' who may or may not be from the house's past, and events take a strange – and ultimately dangerous – turn.

———————

'A deserted house, a grieving girl; the perfect ingredients to take you on a journey between reality and fantasy. *Cicada Summer* makes you believe that anything is possible. My skin prickled, my pulse raced and I couldn't put the book down until I'd finished.' – GLENDA MILLARD

'A treasure of a story, a story to slip into your pocket like a feather or a perfectly round stone – for keeps. Reminiscent of the old-fashioned storytelling I loved as a child, like *Tom's Midnight Garden*, but with a contemporary flavour.' – PENNI RUSSON

cicada summer

kate
constable